the nasties

Chapter 1

Charlie Picker was ten.

Some people said he was big for his age but he didn't feel big now. He felt scared, really scared, and with good reason. The creature was waiting for him and it was bigger than before. He was sure of it. He had seen it out of the corner of his eye as he walked across the park to school. He had seen it watching him from the darkened corner of his room at night when his mum had gone to sleep. It waited with furious patience and a slowly salivating grin. He didn't know exactly what it was, or where it had come from, but that grin told him everything he needed to know. It wanted to kill him and eat him.

A few years ago one of these creatures had found its way into the bathroom of his old house. His screams had brought his dad crashing up the stairs and before he had even realised what was happening the creature was gone, a dark splash of foul liquid running thickly down the tiled wall the only evidence it had ever existed. His dad had wiped the filth away with one of the fluffy bath towels, smearing streaks down the tiles. He had looked at him carefully. Although his eyes were shrouded by the steam on his glasses, Charlie could tell he was judging his reaction.

'No-one else can see it, Charlie, just you and me.' His dad had grimaced for comic effect as he tossed the soiled towel to the floor. 'I think I'll put this in the washing bin.' Noticing the look of alarm on his face, he had quickly continued, 'Don't worry, Mum won't be able to see it. It'll be like it never happened. It's our secret,' he finished with a small grin.

Charlie had been seven at the time. Plenty old enough to feel relief and gratitude, even if he didn't really know what had happened. He just remembered smiling up at his dad, grateful he had been there when the creature forced its way out of the bath tap, like a thick hairy liquid, forming magically into a gnashing and whirling set of fangs. His dad had made him safe. He always had done. But Dad wasn't around anymore. Something had come and taken him. Whatever it was must have been a lot bigger than the creature that had appeared in the bathroom. He thought it had killed him, but didn't know for sure. One thing was certain. He hadn't seen his dad for three years, and he still heard his mum cry herself to sleep at night.

Charlie and his mum lived in a small terraced house on Albert Road in a sleepy market town called Therwick. They had lived in a bigger house with a much larger garden when his dad had still been around. But that felt like a lifetime ago now. He remembered the pain in his mum's face when they left the big house. They couldn't afford to stay, she had explained tearfully to him. The house wasn't really theirs, they were buying it in small chunks, but even these small chunks were too big now it was only his mum's job that was paying for it. He had learnt that all insurance companies were crooks. His mum had said that a lot, to anyone who would listen. They wouldn't give her the money they needed to stay in the big house. They said his dad was missing, not dead, so they wouldn't pay them anything. It was weird how after this Mum went from saying Dad couldn't be gone, to saying he was. Either way, he thought insurance sounded like a waste of money.

If any one of the people who had passed through his house in those frantic first days after his dad vanished had bothered to ask him, he could have given them some clues, or at least a place to start. But they hadn't – no-one had asked him anything specific, just if he was OK, and well that was just stupid, of course he wasn't OK, how could he be? He didn't suppose they would have listened to him anyway. He was just a kid and in truth had been too scared to speak to the policemen who had come to the house in the days after his dad had gone missing.

If he had done, he would have said they should have had a closer look under the shed at the end of the garden. That was where Dad had gone that day. He had been distracted and worried looking, muttering about how he had to go to the thin place, whatever that was. Before he went outside he had told Charlie that he had to stay where he was and not follow him. To wait until he came back, and if not to watch TV until Mum came home. He had nodded. His dad had held him tightly and he had wondered what the big deal was, it only looked like he was going down the end of the garden, not to the outer space or something. But he always did what his dad said, and so he was still sitting in front of the TV when his mum had got home. That was at least three hours after Dad had gone outside. By then he wasn't really watching the brightly coloured images flickering across the screen. All he could think about was when he was going to hear the rattle of the back door as his dad returned to say everything was alright and did he want to have something to eat.

His mum had seemed furious at first. But that hadn't lasted long. She had quickly begun to look scared. He had started to cry, but no-one noticed. He was scared too. He sat on the sofa, with the light of the TV picking out the tears that ran slowly down his cheeks, as his mum became increasingly frantic in her attempts to contact his dad. He was not answering his phone, he wasn't at work or with Bash in the pub or at the golf course. Why the hell would he have left Charlie all on his own? He was seven, for God's sake, his mum had nearly screamed down the phone.

3

The days without his dad turned into weeks and months. He didn't feel he could talk about what he knew, about the monsters and things. Dad had always said it was their secret. His mum cried a lot. He cried too, but mainly because seeing her cry made him want to as well. His dad had said that he was special, that he could see things that other people couldn't. Because of that he needed to be brave. After the incident in the bathroom, his dad had promised he would explain it all to him properly one day. When he was a little older. To teach him stuff that would help. But no-one could explain it to him now he was gone.

The only good thing was that the dark things that moved around the house, and seemed to gather, watching them, had disappeared when his dad did. It was like he had taken them away with him and he was glad about this if nothing else. Even when his dad was here the things he had been seeing scared him.

The ache he felt when he thought about his dad had faded with time, but very slowly. He heard people say it was like a physical pain. A wound that needed to heal. But every now and again the scab was ripped off and the blood flowed afresh. It kept getting snagged on his memories. Like the other week, when he had been tidying his room and had pulled out the box of plastic soldiers from under his bed. The last time he had played with them he had been lying on the floor with Dad, carefully constructing a battle, looking across at his smiling face. The dust on the box spoke the truth of how long it had been since he had gone. The little plastic soldiers looked silly in his hand, but when he had been with his dad they had come alive.

He knew he had to be brave, his mum needed him to be grown up, all of her friends said as much. He was the man of the house now. But he didn't want to be. That was the trouble with being big for his age. Everyone assumed he was older and more in control than he was. He just wanted to feel his dad's arms around him, and smell the clean scent of that stuff he used to put on after he had a shave. He had sneaked the bottle of it out of the bin when Mum had cleared out all of Dad's things. Occasionally he would put a bit of it on his pillow. It brought back powerful memories, mostly good, but he didn't like to do it too often in case the effect wore off.

When they had moved to the house on Albert Road, his mum had seemed better. She seemed less worried, and started to be a bit more like a mum again. The house was smaller but it was just the two of them and because it was an old house, it had a long winding garden that he loved. His room was great as well. It looked out over the garden and he could watch the squirrels jumping across the gap between the two big trees at the end.

Charlie had lived in Therwick all his life. He knew his mum had been born here, but his dad came from further away. They had met at university and ended up living back where his mum had grown up. He liked it here. He liked the fact that the shops were not far away and there was a park to play in. He liked the woods that bracketed the town like two green hands clasped tightly around the houses where everyone lived. It was a good place even though he missed his dad.

He had been encouraged to go to a special group after school to 'help him cope'. There was lots of talk about 'helping him to cope' when his dad disappeared. The answer seemed, by consensus, to be in the school hall on Wednesday evenings, when a lady called Esther would help the assembled children of the area 'COME TO TERMS' with loss. Lots of the things Esther talked about seemed to be in capital letters. He had been going to her group for a long time. He didn't think he was any closer to understanding what loss was, or more importantly how he would find his dad again, but everyone seemed to think it was a good idea that he carried on going. It wasn't a nice place to be. He had, by now, heard more than his fair share of stories of mums, dads, brothers and sisters that had died or left for one reason or another. He felt a bit of a fraud in truth. He knew his dad wasn't 'gone' in the same way as the others and he couldn't speak about it truthfully. He had to sit there, like an actor, while real life played out around him.

Deciding that discretion was the way forward, he kept his real thoughts to himself. He was, in Esther's view, 'making progress in establishing the boundaries of his grief'. He wasn't sure what this meant, but the explanation seemed to make his mum happy and so that was fine with him. Even so he would have preferred not to have to listen to the various stories about how someone's mum or dad got ill and died. It seemed to him there was only so much that could be solved by talking. At some point you needed to get on with some doing, he reasoned.

The other problem with group night was it meant he had to come home after everyone else had left school. It was later and so the hustle and bustle of all the kids and parents was gone. This meant the walk along the path alongside the park back to his house was longer and quieter than it was when he walked home with his friends. There was no joking or laughing, no pushing and shoving, just him, head down, hands in pockets, walking as fast as he could without it being obvious he was nearly running. He knew big boys didn't run. Heroes didn't run. They walked with purpose, like they had the world in a headlock. That's what he wanted to look like, not some scurrying little kid.

But on these evenings the trees in the park seemed bigger and more threatening than they usually did. When it was windy they creaked and groaned, and he would feel a flush of heat creeping up his back and his heart quickening in his chest. At those times he wished his mum didn't have to work so late so she could meet him.

It was on one of his walks back, about four weeks ago now, that he had seen a creature again.

Although it had been a long time since he had last seen one, its movement caught his attention immediately, like his eye was trained to pick it out, an instinctive recognition seemingly beyond his control. His heart had literally stopped beating in his chest. For a terrible moment he was sure it wouldn't start again, but it had, with a great big beat that had left him feeling dizzy and sick. The creature had slithered along the branch of a tree, a fluid streak of midnight. It was shapeless, alien and horrible. In its centre patterns whirled and shifted. It moved silently across the branches between the trees, not like the squirrels that leaped joyfully at the end of his garden. Instead it was like watching a giant leech stretch sightlessly across the gap, securing a foothold and flowing without a sound after it. It looked just like the thing that had come out of the bath tap all those years ago. But it was bigger, and without his dad, without anyone to help, it was much scarier.

He had kept walking. Faster and faster, his legs brushing against each other with a swooshing sound as he desperately tried not to look back over his shoulder. If he didn't look it would go away, he had thought, the age-old remedy used by children when all else failed. But his head had turned, as if on a hinge. He was so tense he could feel the tendons in his neck creak. It was still there.

His walk evolved into a skipping jog. He had been sure the creature was almost above him, in the dense branches of the cluster of trees that grew at the end of the path, as it turned up to his street. Whimpering softly, he felt the sounds start to feed his panic as he heard the creak of something moving directly above him. He started to run blindly, arms flailing as he burst around the corner, straight into the arms of Mrs Olson who lived at the far end of his road. He had screamed. Mrs Olson did too.

'Charlie, whatever is the matter?' she said as she recovered from the shock of him almost knocking her off her feet. Her eyes were wide and she planted her hands theatrically on her chest. He looked back over his shoulder. Again his eye found the creature as it faded slowly back into the shadows around the trunk of a tree. It flickered within a rolling blackness that shrank down and vanished into the shadows. He turned back to her.

'Nothing,' he stammered. 'Just in a rush to get home. Sorry,' he cried, scuttling down the street as quickly as he could.

His hands were still shaking as he turned the key in the front door, and his heart didn't return to its normal rhythm until he had drunk a glass of juice and sat down in front of the TV.

When his mum got home he had hugged her tightly almost as soon as she walked through the door. She hugged him back, with a slightly bewildered look on her face, before peeling him off her and carrying her bags of shopping though to the kitchen. She always thought he was more sensitive after group night, but Esther had said this was a good thing, it meant some of the difficult stuff he was dealing with was coming out, and that was the idea.

The creature started appearing in his bedroom about two weeks after he had seen it on his walk home. He didn't know how it had got in, but figured it didn't need a key or an open window. Monsters always found a way in.

Charlie's bedroom was what might politely be described as 'boy tidy', which meant that if you were lucky you might just find what you were looking for if you stumbled over it in one of the many piles of abandoned clothes, books and forgotten projects. A few months ago his mum had decided that it would be good for him to learn to tidy up after himself. She was tired of picking up after him and had incorrectly concluded that if he was left to his own devices he would soon realize that it was better to keep his room clean. As a result his room was now locked in an eternal spiral of mess and muddle. His mum had taken to extracting what she needed to clean from the piles of clothes and leaving the rest pretty much alone. It was when one of the piles of clothes had begun to move that he realized the creature was in his room.

It had been a Friday evening. He finished cleaning his teeth, spitting enthusiastically into the sink, the white foam spraying against the taps and cup that held his own and his mum's toothbrushes. Swiping at the mess with his hands, he rubbed a towel quickly across his face and pulled the cord that turned the light off with a loud click-clack. A quick step across the narrow landing and he was in his room. His mum's room was at the front of the house, overlooking the narrow street. There was an orange glow from the streetlamp outside the house that reached as far as his door, but the back of the house was dark. He could hear his mum rattling plates in the kitchen below him. A minute or two later, the soft clunk of the fridge door followed by the splash and gurgle of his mum pouring herself a drink. He sat up in his bed and picked up one of the many books that were stacked on the floor. He usually read a book in bed, one of the many he had read a hundred times before, the familiar words helping him to drift off to sleep. The soft burble of the TV started and his eyes started to slide shut. Within five minutes he was asleep, the book hanging loosely from his hand.

He had awoken with a start, about four hours later, his heart beating fast, as if he had woken from a bad dream. His door was shut, and he could tell his mum must be in bed as there wasn't any light casting up the stairs from below. The room was still, the familiar shapes of his wardrobe and desk pulling into focus as, slightly disorientated, he strained to make sense of where he was. He reached across to his clock, pushing the button on the top down, seeing a muted 2 am flash briefly up on the screen. With a sigh, he had pushed himself back down under the covers and closed his eyes against the soft warmth of his pillow. He was beginning to feel himself relax, his heart beat slowing, no longer swishing loudly in his ears, when he had heard a noise. So quiet, but somehow deliberate, the gentle scratch of what sounded like claws.

He had frozen, the hairs rippling across the back of his neck, standing to attention one by one like soldiers on parade. Turning over slowly in his bed he looked across to the wardrobe in the corner of his room. The pile of clothes that had been balancing precariously on the top shifted. Mouth dry, and heart beating faster and faster, he stared at the dark shape that began to move carefully across the top of the wardrobe, displacing another item of clothing which dropped with a soft flump to the floor. It was here, in his house. He knew straight away, even before the strange spiralling shape began to form above him.

Charlie could feel hate pouring from the creature. It made the air in his room feel thick and fetid, like the air in a long neglected cellar. There was a smell as well, growing in intensity, the smell you got when you drove past some road kill on a hot summer day. Sweet and terrible, pushing its way uninvited up your nostrils. He couldn't help it, he screamed. The next thing he saw was his mum stumbling, bleary eyed and half asleep, into his room. She flicked his light on, dazzling him, but not before he saw a dark shape oozing back through the doorframe as she hugged him into her shoulder. 'Did you have a bad dream, Charlie?' his mum asked as she gently stroked his hair. He nodded, pushing his face deep into her skin. 'Can you stay in here tonight, Mum?' he had asked, his face reddening in shame. 'I, I don't feel so great.' His mum sighed. Switching off the light she got into bed next to him, asleep within moments. He lay stiffly next to her, sure he would lie there awake until morning, but after a time he too had fallen into a thin troubled sleep.

His alarm had woken him at 7 am. The space in the bed next to him was empty and cold. His mum had gone to work. He hated that his mum had to get to work so early, and he missed her even more that particular morning. The house seemed very quiet, the silence unusually threatening.

After that first sighting, he had stopped walking along the path, but going the other way around took much longer and he was never ready in time to spare the extra ten minutes it added to his journey. After a week or so he realised he barely gave it any thought as he dashed to school. It was amazing (and a little odd) what you could get used to. He wasn't sure this had anything to do with being 'special' like his dad had said. It was just the way of the world. After all lots of weird things happened, loads of changes that you would never think you could deal with, and you just did. You didn't really have a choice. These creatures were like that. It didn't matter if he told himself it was all imaginary, that it wasn't real. It would still turn up and he couldn't stay scared to death forever. From what he could tell the creature seemed to be keeping its distance for now, it wasn't like it had attacked him or anything, at least not yet. He figured it might just be watching him, maybe reporting back to its boss. The important thing was it hadn't used those claws on him, or those teeth. He hoped it would stay that way, that maybe it would go away eventually when it had done whatever it was doing. It wasn't like he could talk to anyone. Dad had told him no-one else could see them. He was on his own.

Although Charlie didn't know it, the creature had been back to his room again after that first night. He hadn't woken as it slid in through the gap in his sash window. It had sat, watching him, hating him, until the grey light of dawn began to show through the gap in his bedroom curtains.

It wanted to kill the boy so badly, but it couldn't, not yet. It was still small and weak. It had found him though, that was the start. The man on the other side of the world had revived it, given it sustenance, but it needed to grow stronger. Travelling here, through the inter world, was draining. It needed to feed and then to spawn, to make others like it. It knew this boy was the one. When the time came it would kill him, but for now patience was required. It would make no more mistakes, no more banishment, no more years in the abyss. It would be ready.

Chapter 2

Mathilda Crook was having a bad morning. She didn't like Wednesdays and so she lay under her covers even though it was now twenty past eight and she should really be dressed and eating her breakfast. Her Auntie Val shouted up the stairs. 'Come down here this minute, young lady,' she called. 'I'm running out of patience and you're going to be late. I'm not explaining this to the school again.'

She pulled the covers tighter around her head and groaned. She knew her aunt had already been called into school to explain her absence. More than once in fact. The school had always been sympathetic to her situation. They said they knew she needed some extra support, but it was clear to them both that this patience was wearing thin. It was like sand running through an hourglass. At some point it was going to run out.

She heard her aunt's footfall on the stair and called down to her wearily, 'I'm coming.' Her voice dropped to a mutter. 'Keep your hair on.'

She pulled herself out of bed and padded across the landing to the bathroom. Her long dark hair was knotted and her face was puffy. She was a pretty girl, but wore a look of studied disinterest that made her a scary prospect for any of the boys at school. She pulled a brush roughly through her thick hair whilst cleaning her teeth.

Dressed in her faded school jumper and grey woollen skirt, Mathilda took her packed school bag from Aunt Val who stood in the hall, holding the strap between thumb and forefinger. She smiled back at her weakly as she pulled open the door and headed off. Her aunt stared after her for a while, a tired and slightly worried look on her face. She knew Mathilda was growing up fast. She had already had to deal with much more than any fourteen-year-old should. Valerie did her best with her but hadn't expected to be looking after a teenage girl at her age. She had been the quintessential happy spinster, a neat ordered life of work and gardening that had kept her happy and fulfilled. She had never wanted children herself, although she had always enjoyed it when her younger sister had brought Matty (as they had insisted on calling her—no wonder she was a tomboy, she thought) around to visit.

It was a very different type of visit the day the police and social services had arrived with a sobbing Mathilda bracketed in between them. They said it had been an accident. Their car had come off the road and hit a tree. They hadn't stood a chance. So suddenly she had been propelled into a world of childcare and complex emotional support that she had no experience of. Her life had been built around happy solitude. It suited her. People were messy and complicated. They were best experienced in small, manageable doses, and so her life had been constructed to maintain that preference. She tried her best and loved Matty (Mathilda, she corrected herself) as well as she could, but the last eighteen months had been hard for her. To her shame, she felt a sneaking sense of relief when Mathilda turned the corner and was out of sight.

The door to the main entrance of Mathilda's school was wide open. Through it poured a noisy and animated horde of children, shouting and laughing, calling to each other, furiously texting their last messages before phones had to be tucked into bags and pockets. She walked up the steps, head down. Her heavy fringe covered her face. It would be easy to call her a bit of a loner and leave it at that, but that wasn't the whole truth. She had always been a popular and happy girl, not one of the really popular girls, but she had been OK. She had been content with her place in the scheme of things. She was just ordinary, and that was fine. Things had changed. Even though her friends remained, calling 'Hi' to her and asking her to join them in the large courtyard at lunch time, she preferred her own company these days. She always said thanks (it paid to be polite, she thought), but she usually sought out her own space. When she did sit with them, as she often felt she should and occasionally had the strength to actually do, she found herself adrift from the manic flow of conversation about the latest music, fashion, the current 'hot' boy. It all seemed a little pointless. She was sad that she had lost touch with some of the things she had enjoyed so much before her parents had gone.

Her Auntie Val was great, if a little old-fashioned in her ways, but she couldn't see the shape of her life without her mum and dad. It just wasn't right.

Her parents had always been best friends, even she could see that. So much so that on occasion she had felt a little like a plus one in their lives. A welcome addition, but an addition nonetheless. That wasn't to say she didn't feel loved and wanted, but just not as much perhaps as they loved and wanted each other. There were worse things, she figured. She had lots of friends whose parents couldn't stand each other, or at least that was it always looked like anyway. She tried not to overdo the self-analysis. Where would it take her, she thought? It wouldn't bring them back, that was for sure. She had decided that patience was the key. She was waiting for something to happen. For the next change to come. She had coped with the loss of her mum and dad and the resetting of her life with Auntie Val, but she was sure there must be more to it than just this. If she hung in there something would happen, or she would find the energy to make something happen, whatever came first.

Wednesdays were tough, with double maths in the morning and French just after lunch. Thankfully the afternoon was better, with PE taking her through to three o'clock and home time. Mathilda enjoyed PE. She was naturally athletic and had been in the netball and hockey team, always keen to show her mum and dad how good she was at the various tournaments they had ferried her to and from. She now preferred solitary pursuits.

Fortunately this term they had started archery. Everyone had been very excited when they found out. It sounded dangerous and the boys in her class confidently predicted they would be the best shots. She could remember, with a small glow of pleasure, her teacher's stunned expression when on only her second attempt she had brushed her fringe back from her face and effortlessly fired her three arrows in a neat circle around the bright gold centre of the target. She was the only one who had even managed to hit the large straw-backed target that Mr Jones had carefully paced out across the field, as her class lined up in the bright spring sunshine. It was so easy for her. The bow had just felt right in her hands. The feeling of release when she could just concentrate on the arrow and the target, when nothing else mattered for a few small moments, was priceless. Mathilda wasn't sure anyone could have understood this, but she was sure her mum and dad would've approved. They had wanted her to be independent, fearless even. She was determined not to let them down.

As the weeks passed Mr Jones had said that with some more practice she could compete for the county if she wanted to. By that time she thought she could probably compete at that level now, she was already shooting at seventy meters, which was the distance for adults. Mr Jones had set her up her own target and she wanted to beat her best score this afternoon. He had said she could become a Junior Master Bowman and that sounded pretty good to her.

The only downside to archery was the time flew by so fast. Before she knew it Mr Jones was shouting across the field for her to pack up for the day.

Mathilda pulled back the taut bowstring, her three fingers safely enclosed in the brown leather archery glove they all had to wear. Her eyes narrowed as her hand pulled cleanly all the way back to the corner of her mouth. The bowstring whistled slightly in the breeze that chased across the school field. She released and watched as the arrow flew straight and true, punching into the target with a satisfying thump. 'Bullseye'...she whispered with a smile. The boys struggling over on the shorter range looked over as she walked to the target and retrieved her arrows. Her hair blew about her face in the quickening wind. The other girls in the class noticed the boys noticing her too, but she was oblivious.

By the time she had got changed and started walking across town to her old school, the wind was really strong. The trees along the park lurched from side to side as sudden gusts roared through the branches. The early spring leaves were shredded and fell like green confetti around her.

Mathilda walked onwards, head down, her eyes watering. Her old school was quiet, with only a few cars left in the small tarmac carpark by the climbing frame. She could see the lights were on in the main hall. Through the glass she saw the heavy shape of the group counsellor as she reached up and closed the top of the large glazed window that looked out over the playground. She had only been coming to these sessions for about four weeks and this was the main reason she now hated Wednesdays.

It had been her aunt's idea. She had brought up the idea of her talking to someone about what had happened. Mathilda thought she might have read something about child psychology in a Sunday supplement of her newspaper. She also thought one of the reasons was it would mean her aunt didn't have to talk about anything important with her. Feelings weren't really her aunt's thing. She could fix you some dinner, maybe mend a jumper or something, but sit her down and try to talk about how you were feeling and she would run a mile. She understood. None of it was fun for anyone. After all her aunt had lost her little sister so she was pretty sad too, but she really didn't see how these meetings were going to help. She had thought it all through and in her opinion no amount of talking with strangers was going make any difference. Words didn't bring anyone back, they didn't rewind the clock. She couldn't stand the woman who ran the sessions either.

Charlie was sitting in the first chair of the small semi-circle that arced around Esther. They had been talking, or rather Esther had been talking and they had been listening (or at least pretending to), for nearly half an hour. He shuffled uncomfortably on the hard plastic seat. He was too big for these chairs now, they had all outgrown them, except for maybe Peter, who was easily the smallest boy in his class. He thought the new girl, Mathilda, looked even more uncomfortable than he did, even though she was probably only a little bit taller than him. There were five of them in the room tonight. Mathilda was the oldest, then there was Charlie from year six, Luke from year five and the twins from year three, Katie and Owen.

Outside the sky was starting to thicken towards evening. The wind had dropped but the trees still swayed back and forth, casting dancing shadows across the room when the low sun broke through the scudding clouds. In the middle of the room, on a much bigger and more comfortable chair, sat Esther. Although no-one was saying anything, she still felt compelled to bring her finger up to her lips and loudly shush, whilst smiling indulgently. Charlie thought she looked like a fat toad eyeing up a particularly tasty fly. He studiously avoided her gaze. He didn't want to speak tonight. He switched off, allowing his mind to wander. In the background, like a low hum, Esther continued her now familiar speech on 'recognising sadness'. *Straight of out of the textbook, this one,* Charlie thought, he must have heard it a dozen times. He looked out of the window. Her words continued to tumble over each other in a soft drone. Around the room, heads began to drop.

There was something moving within the shadow cast by the fence that surrounded the school. The creature seemed to be much bigger now. Charlie wondered how it had grown so much since the last time. *What was it eating?* he thought with a shudder. He watched as it peeled away from the shadows and started to move stealthily through the longer grass towards the school playground. Another smaller one followed, and then another. They blurred and flickered, in and out of sight, stuttering across the field towards the school. The largest creature appeared at the head of the pack, shifting into a myriad shapes as it crept forward. He was mesmerized. What the hell were these things? What did they want with him?

'Charlie Picker, are you with us this evening?' asked Esther. Her voice rose sharply towards displeasure. He jerked back in his chair, tearing his eyes away from the movement outside the window.

'I, I'm sorry, Esther,' Charlie stammered in reply. 'I was thinking about something.' It still felt odd calling Esther by her first name, but she had insisted, although he was sure that secretly she didn't like it.

'Well that's nice, but can you concentrate please. I'm not here for my own benefit, you know,' she replied, with characteristic lack of patience.

She narrowed her eyes and stared reproachfully at Charlie. There was something about this boy that she didn't like. In fact she wasn't that keen on a number of the children in this room, although being a 'professional' she prided herself on being able to put to one side her personal feelings. This skill had been emphasised very strongly in her training, although secretly she thought they made a bit of a fuss about it. Some kids just needed some straight talking. She looked around the room once more, making eye contact with each child in turn, smiling what she thought was her most pleasant, relaxed smile. The new girl was ignoring her as well. There was no chance of meeting her eyes with all that hair in the way, she thought. She preferred speaking to their parents (well, not parents for this lot, guardians, wasn't it, she thought uncharitably). They treated her with more respect and listened to her properly. The children just seemed to ignore her.

'Well let's get back on track then,' she continued. She cast a final look around the room, trying for inclusive but getting exasperated. She asked Owen and Kate to talk a bit about what they had been doing that weekend. Charlie looked back out of the window. The field and playground were empty again.

He turned his head back to the room and tried his best to concentrate on what Owen was saying. His head began to nod, the combined effect of the heavy heating and Esther's voice acting like a sedative.

The large window behind Charlie suddenly reverberated with a massive thump. He jumped up from his chair with a grunt of surprise. Splayed across the window was the furiously grinning creature. It flickered and buzzed against the glass, its shape so contorted that his eyes couldn't make sense of it. Esther, Luke, Katie and Owen were all staring at him.

'What is it now, Charlie? Please sit down so Owen can finish what he was saying,' said Esther. Her voice was brittle with barely contained anger.

He stammered and looked wildly around the room. He had never seen anything like this before. Not for the first time he silently cursed his luck at being left with this 'power'. A power to see monsters no-one else could. A power to be constantly scared, like your nerve endings were on fire, fizzing with tension for what might come next – *thanks, Dad*, he thought bitterly.

The creature moved against the glass, causing it to flex ever so slightly. He was close to losing it, when he noticed that Mathilda was also staring open-mouthed at the window. Her round face was pale and grey with shock. She looked over at him in disbelief before her eyes returned to the dark shape that covered most of the bottom pane of the window. It had stretched itself out flat against the glass. You could see the skin pulsating, a thick heavy movement that reminded him of the way the maggots wriggled in the bait boxes of fishermen by the canal in summer, a sort of furious boiling movement of flesh. It was horrible. Mathilda's nerve broke.

'W-w-what is that thing?' she cried, staring at Esther.

'What are you taking about?' replied Esther, anger staining her voice, her training forgotten. 'What are you two up to? If this is a joke then it is neither funny nor appropriate. Sit down at once, you are scaring Katie and Owen.'

'Can't you see it?' cried Mathilda.

'See what?' she replied. She stood up and advanced towards her. 'All I can see is you two disturbing my group, now please sit down.'

Charlie cast a despairing look at Mathilda. He forced himself back down on his seat.

'I am going to count to three, Mathilda,' she said. 'After that I will expect to see you sat back down in your chair. You will be calm.'

Esther started to gather her composure. Swallowing deeply and forcing a horribly unconvincing smile to her face, she continued. 'This is a difficult place for us all, I get that,' she said, warming to this caring, empathetic persona, 'but I expect you to be calm when we have our discussions. We don't interrupt. We listen with respect, yeah. That's one of the most important rules of our group,' she went on.

Mathilda barely registered any of this. Her eyes were fixed on the creature that peeled itself off the window. It reformed into a feline-like shape. To her horror its head suddenly split open, turning in on itself like an umbrella in the wind. A vicious grin, filled with needle teeth, burst out of the fleshy red blob that had been its head. It tottered about for a minute before it vanished with an audible pop, the air rushing back into the space it had occupied.

'Oh my God,' she said weakly. 'It's gone, right?' Her legs felt rubbery and she didn't feel like she could stand. 'You saw it, didn't you, Charlie? I saw that you saw it.' Her voice rose suddenly, almost a scream. 'What was it?'

Esther's large face had turned a blotchy red, and her small piggy eyes seemed to bulge ever so slightly out of her face. In that moment, it briefly occurred to

Charlie that she was almost as scary as the thing that had been on the window. 'That's it. I would like both of you to leave please,' she said in a strangled voice. 'There is no place for this behaviour in my group, I will be speaking to your teachers and your parents, I mean guardians, oh whatever, I'll be speaking to someone about this.'

She stood, shaking slightly, in the middle of the circle of chairs, her finger pointed towards the double doors at the far end of the hall. Charlie considered protesting, looked again at Esther's faintly sweaty face, and thought better of it. Mathilda had already put her coat on and was heading for the door. He followed her, feeling sick at the trouble he was bound to get in, and sicker still that he had to walk home when that thing was outside. Mathilda clearly had the same concern as she was standing in the reception area, looking uncertainly out of the doors that led to a path that ran around the playground and out of the main school gates. She turned round and looked at him. Her face was still pale and she was trembling slightly despite the heavy warmth of the heating. He thought she looked younger all of a sudden. When she had first joined the group she had looked very grown up, much more in control than the rest of them. She had looked pretty cool.

She didn't look or feel cool now, not that she would have considered herself in those terms anyway. What she had seen had burned itself into her mind. When she blinked she could see the last image of the strange and awful creature folding in on itself in a splurge of red flesh. She tried to control her shaking voice.

'What was that, Charlie? Why could we see it and no-one else could?' She looked out of the window again. 'Do you think it's still out there?' she asked urgently

They heard Esther moving around in the hall. Her face, still angry and red, appeared pressed up to the narrow glass panel. She peered through, her eyes narrowing when she spotted them.

'We better go,' he said. 'I think Esther's gone mental. I have seen those things before, but never like that, never so close.' Charlie gulped. 'I thought I was the only one who could.' The relief he felt as he said this was enormous. For the first time in months he didn't feel alone. 'I think they've gone,' he said. 'Did you hear that sound when it disappeared?'

He pulled on his coat and pushed open the door. Mathilda winced and shrank back momentarily, before following him outside. The sky was darkening now.

The shadows across the playing field had disappeared with the setting sun. 'Where do you live, Charlie?' she asked.

'Albert Road. It's just up behind the park. I usually walk up the path over there. It doesn't take that long, but, er it might be a bit, I don't know, quiet that way now.'

Mathilda nodded. 'I live on the Ridgeway,' she said. 'I think it might be better if we both go the long way home tonight, don't you think, through town? There'll be more people about.'

Charlie smiled slightly 'Not that they'll be able to see anything anyway,' he snorted.

She stared at him thoughtfully. 'No I guess not. Why don't you tell me what you know about all this on the way?'

They walked quickly, nearly running, down the path and out of the school gates. The creatures were nowhere to be seen.

On the way home Charlie told her everything he knew. In truth this wasn't a lot, but even so they had to slow down so he could finish his story before they got to the end of Albert Road. Even before they'd got to town, her mind was whirling. She hadn't even noticed the sniggers and catcalls from some kids in her year who were hanging around the town park. They had watched her walking past with Charlie. 'New boyfriend, Mathilda?' they shouted. She was oblivious. She listened carefully as he spoke in a quiet but steady voice.

'These things, they've been following me for a while, I don't know, about a month. They just turned up out of nowhere. There was just one at first, but now there are more. I don't know where they come from, but, well it's complicated, but my dad did tell me about them.'

'Your dad,' said Mathilda. 'What's he got to do with all this?'

'He knew about them. He could see them like we can, my mum can't. In fact most people can't. They're some sort of special monster. I reckon they hate me because I can see them. That's why they're following me. Dad said they eat children.' He looked at her disbelieving face. 'It's true. He said they eat kids, it's what makes them strong. Dad told me this stuff just before, well, before he disappeared.'

'You don't talk about that much at the group, what happened?' asked Mathilda.

'It's difficult to explain, he gone, but not dead, actually I'm not really sure what he is, but he's not around anyway. It's just me and Mum. But these things, they're around...' Charlie stopped talking for a moment. 'I think they might have been around for a long time, even back when I was just a baby. Maybe I've always been able to see them.'

He thought very hard and although he did not entirely trust the memory, his dragged it up, old and shaky. 'You know the park, the bit that's fenced off for the little kids?' Mathilda nodded. She knew it, her mum and dad had pushed her on the swings many times when she was tiny. She remembered yelling for them to push her higher and faster.

'I reckon I was about three or four. Mum and Dad had taken me there. I was sat in a pushchair or something. There was this thing, a creature, hanging from the climbing frame in the playground. I remember there had been other kids in the play area, running around on that funny spongey floor that makes you feel like you're walking on the moon. None of them could see it, but it was watching them. It was sniffing at the air, like it was smelling something good. The kids must have known it was there somewhere, they must have sensed it because they never ran anywhere near the climbing frame. It scared me. I think I started to cry. Mum had thought I wanted to go on the climbing frame. I think my Dad was able to make it go away. He could see it, I'm sure of that and he knew I could see it too. Dad had done something. It grinned at us and vanished. That grin stuck with me for a while, I can tell you.'

'Hold on. This is mental. Your dad could see them. But what are they? Where do they come from, Charlie?'

'I don't know,' he replied. 'Dad had only just begun to tell me more about it when he disappeared. He said I was still too young to be told everything, but he said he would make sure I would know what to do when I was older, so I could protect myself. He did say the creatures had been around a long time, like they were as old as the Earth, maybe even older. He sort of said it was his job to know about them, and he had to keep an eye out for them and, you know, go after them if they were scaring anyone. It was all pretty confusing. I thought he worked in London.'

His dad had smiled at his confusion, ruffling his hair. He had ended up saying it wasn't a job, more like a vocation. He didn't think it was worth telling Mathilda that. He still didn't really know what he had meant.

'Ages ago, when I was little, one of those things attacked me, or tried to. It came into our old house, through the bath tap. I was in the bath, it scared the life out of me,' he said with a slight smile.

'You mean it came into your house! You're joking, right?' she said incredulously.

'No joke. I'm not really sure what happened. Dad just closed his hands around it as it was trying to pull itself out of the tap. He kind of squeezed it or something. These weird flames were there for a second and then it was, well, gone.'

He didn't think his explanation really captured the memory very well. The bright blue flames pouring from his dad's hands, the dazzling neon light that increased in intensity, was hard to describe. The creature had been struggling furiously to free itself from the tap, thrashing and flinging itself back and forth right up to the point it had exploded in a splat of dripping blood. His dad had told him that he would teach him how to do the same, how to make the blue flames come, but he never got round to it, and then he had disappeared.

'They must have a name, these things,' Mathilda said.

'Yes, well, sort of. I'm not sure if it's official or anything, but dad called them Nasties.'

'The Nasties,' she repeated, nodding slightly. It was a slightly childish name but it somehow felt right.

'Dad seemed pretty serious when he said it,' he said, his voice a bit defensive. He hadn't smiled or laughed at all, he had been deadly serious.

Mathilda nodded thoughtfully. She had listened with a growing dread that made it harder and harder for her to see how she would be able to dismiss this as a moment of madness, something to be forgotten. 'Your dad's gone,' she said. 'And you don't know anyone else, who can, well, see these things?'

'Yeah, he's gone...' he replied huskily. He stared down at his feet as unexpected tears sprang to his eyes. He didn't want Mathilda to see. 'It's just me.' He looked up at her, blinking. 'And now you.'

Chapter 3

Lottie Peacock was bored. It was a Sunday afternoon and her brother and sister were both out. Worse still her sister, who was only two years older than Lottie, was at a tenth birthday party and her mum had taken her. This meant that Lottie was stuck at home with her dad. He had promised to play with her when she had started protesting about her mum going out for the afternoon, but as soon as they had gone he had settled himself down in the big chair in front of the TV and put on the football. Lottie hated football, it was all her dad and stupid brother ever talked about. What was the point in it all, she thought, it was boring, running around like that. It was OK when you were playing it in the garden and were doing something, but just watching it? Lottie gave up trying to coax her dad out of the chair. When her mum was not around, Dad was a lot better at ignoring her. The last time she went downstairs, she'd counted three empty beer cans stacked next to his chair. Only a short time later she started to hear the soft sounds of his snoring drifting up the staircase.

Lottie had played with her Sylvanians and had fiddled for a little while with her old Gameboy, before dropping it onto her bed and flopping down on the pillow with an exasperated sigh. She didn't really enjoy computer games, and couldn't understand how her brother and sister could sit for hours in front of the screen in her brother's darkened room, furiously bashing buttons. Her mum said she was lucky to be so imaginative, and was better off making up her own games anyway. But there was a limit to how long she could amuse herself. Lottie wished one of her friends from school could have come round to play. After a minute of staring at the fine cracks that spider-webbed across her ceiling, she got up and looked out of the window. It had a view down the long garden at the rear of her house. It was a bright and sunny day, the lawn a dazzling green, bordered by colourful flowers that rambled all the way down to a shaded area under the trees at the end where there was a shed and makeshift pen that enclosed the family rabbit, Flops (on account of his drooping ears). Beyond the garden fence all you could see were trees where Therwick woods started their occupation of the land.

The rabbit had been her sister's birthday present, but she didn't show much interest in him anymore, at least not until Lottie said she wanted to play with him or clean him out. Then she would protest loudly that Lottie was trying to steal her pet. Lottie squinted as she tried to pick out Flops in the heavy shadows. It was darker than usual down there, she thought. She pushed her face closer to the window, the glass steaming up as she breathed out of her nose. She stepped back to wipe it clear, before choosing instead to draw a smiling face. Her finger moved over the glass with a squeak, and within the clear lines cut through the mist, she saw a sudden movement.

There was something down there with Flops. A dark shape was moving along the bottom of the back fence where the ivy grew down in thick streams. She wiped the window quickly, and could see the rabbit sitting towards the front of his pen, close to the chicken wire that fenced him in. If it was a cat or a fox, that would be bad, she thought. She grabbed her favourite rag doll on instinct and turned and ran down the stairs. 'Daddy!' she called. 'There's something in with Flops, please help.' Her dad raised a bleary eye, groaned and turned onto his side in the chair. *Fat lot of use he is*, she thought angrily, and decided to deal with it herself.

The back door opened with a juddering squeal. Another job her dad could have been doing instead of sleeping, Lottie thought. The look on her face, had she known it, was remarkably similar to the one her mother increasingly used when looking at her dad. She pulled on her green wellingtons and ran down the path, the sun bouncing her shadow across the lawn, the rag doll in her hand flopping back and forth. As she approached the trees she slowed down. The bright sunshine dazzled her. She blinked hard at the spots dancing in front of her eyes, and hesitated in front of the shadowed trees. Flops was still there. Behind him she could see a dark cat-like shape sliding along the fence. To her astonishment it seemed to go through the fence, like it was made of smoke.

She rubbed her eyes. Whatever she had seen had disappeared but there was now a smell, and not one she had come across before down the end of the garden. It was not like the smell of Flops' poo, which she was used to and secretly quite liked. This was a heavy, meaty smell, thick and cloying. She decided it might be better to ask her dad for some help and started to turn back to the house. The shed door slowly creaked open behind her. Lottie spun round, her heart racing. The inside of the shed was a pitch black that defied her eyes' attempt to pick out the bits and pieces she knew she should be able to see. Where were her bike and the lawnmower? she thought, leaning forward to try to see.

The dark suddenly lurched out of the shed and closed around her, stifling a scream that formed on her lips. With a guttural snarl Lottie, and whatever had taken her, disappeared, swirling away in a vortex of black.

Her doll lay sightlessly on the mud, the sunshine dappling softly through the leaves, the shadows softened now by the bright spring sunshine. Flops hopped slowly back to his hutch and chewed contentedly on the greens Lottie's mum had thrown in to him that morning. Lottie was gone.

Lottie Peacock was reported missing at six o'clock on Sunday evening. Her mum and dad had looked everywhere when they couldn't find her in the house. They had found her doll at the end of the garden, but that was it. Her dad said she had gone down to check on Flops, but he couldn't remember when. By eight o'clock most of the parents in the street had been out looking for her. They continued the search as the sky darkened. Torchlight cut this way and that in the gathering gloom. Mrs Peacock stayed in the house where she was being comforted by her friends and someone from the police.

Mathilda had heard her aunt talking on the phone, and was surprised when she had pulled on her coat and headed out. She usually watched her soaps on Sunday night. She had told her to lock the door and stay put. She explained that a little girl had gone missing and everyone was going to help find her. She had probably just wandered off, she said, but you had to be careful these days. Mathilda had watched her out of the window as she met up with Mrs. Price from number 27 and headed off into night. She thought of Charlie and all the things they had talked about on Wednesday and again on Friday when they met after school. She had a horrible feeling in her stomach when she thought of the little girl. The Nasties were growing in number. They were seeing them all the time. She couldn't help but think that they had something to do with Lottie. Animals couldn't breed if they didn't have lots to eat, she thought with a shudder. She decided to get back in touch with Charlie the next day after school. If she snuck out of class ten minutes early she would be able to get over to his school before he finished. She could say she had appointment with a doctor or a therapist. That would do the trick. The teachers wouldn't ask any questions, not about that type of thing.

It was frustrating that she didn't have his phone number so she could call him, Mathilda thought, or her own smartphone like all her friends. That would have made life way easier but her aunt always said they were too much money. She had looked around the house the other night for a phone book, but she wasn't sure they even made those anymore. That just left the old-fashioned approach – face to face. She would make sure she saw him tomorrow.

By the time her aunt got home it was very late and Mathilda was asleep on the sofa. She was exhausted. They had looked all over the town, with some of the men venturing out into the woods with flashlights, but no-one had seen Lottie Peacock. She gently shook Mathilda awake, and led her upstairs to bed. It was starting to rain outside and splatters of it hit the window in Mathilda's bedroom. She shuddered and said a small prayer for the lost little girl as she looked out into the empty street.

Chapter 4

Charlie knew it was serious even before Mrs McGildrey had stood up at the special assembly that was called on Monday morning. He had heard the news on the radio that morning and seen the worried look on his mum's face. She had even walked with him to school, despite the fact that she would be late to work. Lottie Peacock had been (*was*, Charlie thought, shuddering) in year four. He didn't know her. Year fours and sixes didn't really mix, but it was a small school and he could picture her face.

The teachers sat around the edge of the hall. The entire school had been gathered together, cross-legged and hushed, looking at the sombre face of Mrs McGildrey who explained that Lottie had gone missing and the police were looking for her. Everyone was worried but the police were looking very carefully she said. He could tell she was choosing her words carefully so she didn't upset the little kids who sat at the front of the hall, but he had heard what the man on the radio said. He had said that Lottie may have been taken by someone. He found it difficult to concentrate for the rest of the day. The lessons about history and science all seemed a bit pointless, even the teachers seemed distracted. Like Mathilda he had a feeling that the Nasties may have had something to do with the disappearance.

He had seen a Nastie every day since last week, when the big one had surprised them at Esther's session. This morning there had been five of them. One, it could only be the first one he had seen, perhaps the one that came into his room, was very large now, about the size of a man, but squat and more powerful looking. The others were smaller but as the days passed it was clear they were all growing in size. They sat like fat crows on a phone line, watching. He had decided he would try to get over to Mathilda's school at home time.

The day dragged on terribly. By the time the hands of the clock inched closer to three o'clock, he was squirming in his seat, desperate to get away in time to catch Mathilda. When Mr Sanders concluded the lesson, he was up and out of his seat so fast that he nearly fell into his desk. 'Careful, Charlie,' said Mr Sanders sternly, as he righted himself and raced out of the doors to the cloakroom.

Despite the sunshine it felt cold outside, and he pulled his coat tightly around himself as he ran down the path towards the school gates. He wasn't really looking where he was going, and didn't see Mathilda standing just to one side of the gate.

'Hey, you,' she called as he hustled past her.

'Oh, thank God you're here,' he blurted out. 'Have you heard what's happened? Do you think this is something to do with the Nasties? There are more and more of them. What are we going to do?'

Mathilda held up her hand. 'Calm down, Charlie,' she said. 'Let's go back to your house and have a think.'

'My house?' he replied uncertainly. 'Why my house?' There was something about the idea of taking her back there that made him feel a bit weird.

'Well we can't go to mine, my aunt is having people round today and your mum's at work. Besides I've got an idea.'

The rest of the children were now making their way out of the building and down to the main gates. More parents than normal hovered about expectantly. His mum had said she couldn't make it to pick him up, something at work she had to do, but she insisted he walk the long way home with one of his friends, and under no circumstances was he to take the alley by the park like he usually did. He was keen to get moving before one of his friends saw him and started asking him why he was hanging out with a girl (even if she was older and looked pretty cool). Even with what was going on, he thought he could do without that. 'OK. Let's get going then,' he said. They walked quickly up the path towards his house.

'You don't see any Nasties at the moment do you?' Mathilda asked as they approached the alley alongside the park. He stopped and looked around. 'No, but they're pretty good at hiding. Do you?'

'No. They're around though. You can kind of feel it, can't you?' she said with a shudder. 'What time will your mum be back?'

'About five. Why?'

'That should give us enough time,' Mathilda said. 'We've got some investigating to do.'

Charlie opened the front door of his house and let Mathilda walk in past him. He looked furtively up the street but there was no-one around. He didn't know why he felt so nervous, but having a girl in his house was a bit unusual for him. More than unusual in fact. Mathilda had slumped down onto the old sofa in front on the TV. It was brown and saggy but still really comfortable. His mum had often talked about replacing it but never had. She didn't look bothered about being here.

'Do you want a drink?' he asked as he walked through to the kitchen at the rear of the house.

'Are you left on your own a lot? Must be cool.'

He hadn't really thought of it like that. He poured himself a glass of juice. He thought it would be cooler to have his dad around, so his mum didn't need to work all the time and they could all be together.

'Are you OK?' Mathilda said. He jumped at the sound of her voice. She was standing directly behind him. 'Sorry, I drifted off for a minute,' he stammered. 'So what's this big idea of yours then?'

Mathilda poured herself a drink and put the carton back in the fridge. She took a sip and pushed her thick fringe out from her eyes as she thought about how to explain her plan.

'I was thinking about what you said the other week when we talked about your dad and how he knew all about the Nasties. You said that he wanted to tell you more about them, to tell you the secrets he knew and about the way he could stop them. You said that he promised he would find a way to make sure you would have all you needed to protect yourself. But he never got the chance to tell you as he was taken.' He nodded. Everything she said made sense, his dad had started to explain things but then he was gone and there was nothing but a whole load of unanswered questions.

Mathilda continued. 'I was watching TV the other night. It was one of the soaps that my aunt watches, and this girl in it had got a load of money after her dad died. A judge or something came and explained to her what she had been left. It was all written down, what she would get and what he wanted her to do with it. She was actually a bit mad, because he didn't want her to do anything fun with it, like buy a flash car or jet off somewhere and mess around on a beach. He wanted her to go to university and train to be a doctor or something. Anyway, that's not the point. It was all set out for her, y' know.'

'But my dad didn't leave us any money. That's why Mum had to sell our house and move here,' interrupted Charlie.

'I wasn't really thinking about money,' she said. 'It's the letter. Don't you see? A letter that said all the things he wanted her to do. I was wondering if your dad might have left you anything like that. I mean it sounds like he wanted to help you. Maybe he planned ahead and left you something after all?'

Charlie stared at her thoughtfully. It was a good idea. He was impressed. The idea that his dad might have left him something, like he could hear his voice and have a part of him with him now, that would be great, but his mum had never mentioned anything, and he thought she would have. Unless of course she didn't want him to know.

'I don't think there is anything. At least Mum's never mentioned it.' He looked at Mathilda's slightly disappointed expression. 'It's still a good idea though. I'll ask her. You never know, she might have been waiting for the right moment to tell me or something.'

'Maybe we could have a look around the house? 'Mathilda persisted. 'Do you know where your mum keeps all the papers and important things? My mum and dad always used to have a box of stuff in the bottom of the wardrobe.'

'I've never looked to be honest,' he said. 'I think I should ask Mum first, I don't want her to come home and find me hunting through her cupboards with a strange girl,' he said with a smile.

'I didn't think I was that strange,' she replied with a grin, but she was disappointed. She had clung to the idea of some guidance from Charlie's dad. It just felt right for some reason. Also she had felt pretty clever last night when she had her flash of inspiration. It was rubbish it hadn't worked out neatly, quickly, like she had hoped. Life wasn't like the TV.

'Fingers crossed,' she said with a smile, 'Your mum might come up with something.'

That night after tea, Charlie brought his mum a cup of coffee as she sat on the sofa. She looked tired and used up. She was definitely doing more hours at work than she used to, he thought. Some days he barely saw her in the morning and then only for an hour or two in the evening, before she either went to bed or fell asleep, exhausted, on the sofa. 'Thanks, Charlie,' she said as he handed her the steaming drink. She clasped both hands around the cup and blew gently on the coffee before taking a birdlike sip.

'Sit down then,' she said, 'tell me about your day.'

Charlie rambled on for a minute or two about school, talking about nothing in particular. He carefully tried to pick the moment to change the direction of the conversation towards his dad. This was always difficult; his mum was always reluctant to talk about him, unless she was in a particularly good mood. The dark circles under her eyes told him that now wouldn't be a good time, but the events taking place meant he had to press on. He moved in closer to her on the sofa, wrapping his arms around her waist. They were both staring at the TV. She couldn't see his face, or hopefully feel how fast his heart was beating. He asked as casually as he could, 'Mum, when Dad went away did you have to see a judge or anything like that?' He felt her stiffen ever so slightly.

'Why do you ask?' she replied.

'Oh, just because we were talking about it at school, a friend said he had seen a judge when his grandma died and they had all got a letter from her to say what she wanted them to do with the money she had left them.' He was starting to sweat slightly. He was speaking too fast, his voice sing-song and unnatural to his ears. He hated lying to his mum and his stomach was fluttering wildly.

'Well there was no money when your dad went, Charlie, I can assure you of that,' she said in a tight voice.

'Was there anything else, did he leave me anything?'

'No,' she replied quickly. 'Nothing. He left us both with nothing.'

He sat up and looked at her. 'I'm sorry, Mum. I didn't want to upset you, I just...'

'It's alright, love,' she said. She got up and flicked off the TV with the remote control. 'I think you better get ready for bed, don't you?'

'OK, Mum. Are you alright? You look a bit angry,' he replied, searching out his mum's face, but she wouldn't look him in the eye as she moved quickly to the stairs.

Charlie couldn't sleep. He heard his mum downstairs pouring herself a glass of wine and she never usually drank during the week. He felt guilty about upsetting her and silently cursed Mathilda for putting the idea in his head.

He had to admit though, his mum had acted a bit odd when he asked. She had jumped when he mentioned a letter. He couldn't stop thinking about what it all meant. His mind was racing as he lay in his bed. A short while later he heard his mum put her glass on the sink and tread carefully up the stairs. He rolled onto his side and closed his eyes, breathing in a long deep rhythm as his mum quietly opened his door to check on him. Satisfied, she moved carefully away from his room and went down the hall to her bedroom. He sat up in his bed and listened. A minute or two later he heard the soft clink and rattle of the loft ladder being pulled down. He carefully got out of bed and tiptoed across his room to the door. Peering out into the hall, he could see his mum's legs going up the ladder as she pulled herself up into the loft.

He had only been in the loft once, when his mum had let him climb the ladder to watch her sorting some stuff out up there. It was an Aladdin's cave of boxes and old bits and bobs that had been stored there since they moved in. Mum kept saying she would have a clear out and get rid of things, but she never did. A square of soft yellow light appeared in the ceiling of the hall as his mum turned on the single bulb that hung from the rafters. He could see her shadow moving across the wall and heard the sound of boxes being moved around.

After a moment the boards creaked and his mum slowly came back down the ladder, carefully holding a small brown wooden box. The ladder was pushed back up and the loft hatch pushed shut with a soft click. The box was on the floor, and from the light cast from his mum's room he could see it was covered in dust. She picked it up and went into her room.

He paused in his doorway, not knowing what to do next. He wanted to see what was in the box. The landing floorboards creaked terribly when you walked on them. It was one of the many jobs that needed doing in the house, his mum said, so he knew he would have to be really careful if he was to get to her door without alerting her. *OK*, he thought, *worst case she hears me and I will just pretend I have had a nightmare or something, that would work.*

He moved carefully across the landing with exaggerated strides. Knowing the worst floorboards were in the middle, he edged along the walls until he was outside his mum's half open bedroom door. He peered carefully through the gap between the door and the frame, barely breathing at all.

His mum was sitting on the bed, the box open at her side. In her hand she held a piece of paper which she was staring at intently. The paper was wrinkled and had yellowing sellotape holding it together, like it had been torn up and put back together at some point. Although he couldn't see her face, he could tell she was crying. On the bed next to the box was a heavy looking chain with a small stone hung on it. From what he could see it was a long letter, but his mum seemed to finish it very quickly, like she knew what it said and just needed to skim over it. With an angry sweep of her arm she scooped up the stone and pushed it back in the box together with the letter. She slammed the lid shut and pushed the box under her bed. He moved carefully back from the door and hurried to his room. He wanted to know what was in the letter. He needed to speak to Mathilda – all these things, but it would have to wait. It was a while before he drifted off to sleep.

At around midnight a black shape formed in the corner of his mum's room. It rose silently up from a gap between the floorboards and swirled into a shape that flickered across the rug towards the bed. She muttered something in her sleep and stirred briefly. The creature was staring intently at the box under the bed, hate pouring from it like a cloud of bitter gas. The box shuddered ever so slightly on the bare wooden floor, a soft rattle followed by a bright blue light cutting out of the ridge that formed the hinged lid. The creature hissed, cat-like, drawing back as if stung. A series of baleful red eyes narrowed and flashed in its twisted shape before it whirled upwards and vanished through the open sash window.

His mum was gone by the time he had got up and started to brush his teeth. All he could think about was the box under her bed. He was worried she might have moved it somewhere else during the night. He went downstairs, pulling his school jumper over his head as he walked and saw his lunchbox on the worktop in the kitchen, together with a scrawled note. *See you tonight*, it said. *Fruit box in the fridge, love Mum xx*. She was gone.

He ran back upstairs to her room and walked carefully around her bed. The curtains were open and bright sunshine poured through. He dropped to his knees and pushed back the sheets that draped over the side of the bed frame. The box was there, pushed back amongst the shoes and other bits and pieces that were stored there. He reached forward and then stopped, his hand hanging in mid-air. For some reason he was scared, he didn't want to open the box alone. He didn't want to read the letter without someone with him. He decided to go and get Mathilda. It had been her idea after all.

Mathilda was listening to the radio as she ate her cereal. The DJ had sombrely mentioned that Lottie Peacock was still missing and the search had been extended to the surrounding woods. Her mum had made a tearful appeal for information on the news last night. Her dad stood ashen-faced and silent next to his sobbing wife, his hand hovering over but not quite touching her shoulder. The newsreader confirmed that the police were calling in experts to help with the search. They had watched the footage silently, her aunt shaking her head in despair.

She wondered how Charlie had gotten on with his mum as she packed her bag and got ready to leave. He might have bottled it, she thought. He had looked nervous about asking her.

'Bye,' she called as she swung her bag over her shoulder and opened the door.

'Be careful, Matty,' Val replied. 'Come straight home after school and don't hang around anywhere on your own.'

'I will,' she said as she shut the door and started walking to school. It was all too much, she thought. This was big stuff, maybe too big for a couple of kids to handle. She wondered with her head down to the end of her road. The novelty of being part of this mystery, if it ever had been a novelty, was wearing off.

'Mathildaaaaa.'

She heard her name and turned to see Charlie running up her street towards her. He was red-faced and breathing heavily when he stopped in front of her, hands on his knees.

'I—I'm glad I caught you,' he gasped between breaths. 'I think there's something from my dad. We need to go back to my house now and see.'

They sat together on the edge of his mum's bed. Charlie had partly drawn the curtain and the room was in shadow. He had never bunked off school before and was nearly as nervous about that as what may or may not be in the small wooden box on his lap. Carefully he opened the box and gently lifted out the folded pieces of paper within. The paper was nothing special, just old lined A4, but it had been carefully reconstructed with sellotape which ran this way and that across the pages like cracks in a mirror. The handwriting was familiar. He had seen it on the old birthday cards he kept in a box in the cupboard in his room. The writing was his dad's. He smoothed out the three pages and started to read. His heart was beating so loud he was sure Mathilda must be able to hear it. As they read the first line, she put her hand carefully on his arm. He didn't notice.

Dearest Charlie

I had a friend hold this letter and package and promise to send it to you if I ever disappeared. It's odd writing like this but if you are sat there reading it then I must have gone.

I know a letter is a bit old-fashioned, you've probably never been sent one before, but there was no other way. It's been a long time since I've written one myself. I hope you can read my handwriting.

I have thought hard about what I should say to you in this letter and it has been very difficult for me to write. Much of what is in here was passed on to me by my own dad – but I was fortunate enough to be much older and have the benefit of him telling me in person, which meant a lot of the more challenging stuff I have to say was easier for him to explain. I will do my best.

It is important that you are brave when you read what I have to say. It is also important that you read the letter very carefully. What I will tell you may save your life.

I am afraid Mum can't help you with this. Mum is great, but she never understood or believed in the things I need to explain to you now, not that I can blame her. It does sound a bit crazy. Trust me, Charlie. Follow what I say and you'll have every chance of surviving what will come, I only wish I were there with you to keep you safe and teach you what you need to know.

The creatures you have seen since you were a small baby are very real. I told you they were called the Nasties, but that's not their real name. The one I heard the most from my dad, your Grandad, was Kerberos. I think this is something to do with demons, but I am not sure they have anything to do with a heaven or a hell either. I wish I had paid a bit more attention. I was never a great listener but I will tell you what I remember.

Granddad said they have been around since the world was young, maybe before then, before everything. They are the cruellest and most foul creatures to have walked this Earth. They live in the shadows, we don't really know where, but they seem to hide away, somewhere between our world and all the others. They don't think like we do. They don't seem to know anything but their own hunger, which is insatiable. The old records said that the Kerberos have been pillaging the Earth for centuries. They feed on what we care for the most – our children. I know I am skipping around a lot here, Charlie – I am scribbling this down in a rush, so sorry if it is all over the place. I just need to tell you as much as I can.

As you know, most people can't see the Nasties – I will call them that, it's easier somehow. I don't know why this is the case and why we are different. It's all a bit hazy but Granddad explained it to me this way. He said that all living things are meant to have a counter balance in the universe. So a bird might eat a worm and a hawk might then eat a bird. It all works out up the food chain. I'm sure you will have learnt about this at school. It's the way the world works – real circle of life stuff. The Nasties are from outside the normal order of things. They are from before, long, long, ago when the universe was populated by all sorts of strange and dark creatures. The world was a very different place. Not like what you read in books. It was a place of nightmares, where monsters existed – visiting the young Earth from other places, searching for food. The Earth grew older and after a while people evolved, climbing out of the trees and caves, becoming more like we are now. People are complex, full of fear and love and all those things. It made them taste good to the Nasties. Fear made them taste the best of all and children, well children just topped the lot. And so they fed and fed. No-one could see them, no-one could stop them. They grew in size and number. We think they would have finished off people altogether if it were not for the fact that whatever controls the universe likes balance and that meant something had to happen to hold the Nasties back. Granddad said we were that something, Charlie, or at least our ancient ancestors were. A type of person with the power to see these creatures and fight them. We are born of those people, Charlie, me and you, we are from the Nephilim, the Watchers. We are descended from these first families and have the power to kill them.

You will remember that night when the Nastie came through the bath tap and the flame that I pushed into it. It made a bit of a mess! You might not believe it but you can do that too. It is in your blood. The power to do it runs through you, you just need to learn how to set it free.

With this letter I have enclosed an amulet. It might not look much (I remember thinking the same when granddad gave it to me) but it is really important and very powerful.

Think of it like a key, when you put it on (I know it's on a chain and you won't want to wear a necklace – but stick with me), it will allow you to access the power that's in you. It's this power and the way you will be able to control it that will help you to kill a Nastie. It's also going to protect you.

When you are wearing it you will be safe. The Nasties won't be able to kill you. It will make you strong, so don't take it off OK. Keep it on always.

They stopped reading and looked down into the box at the grubby looking chain and small grey stone that was attached to it by a piece of twisted metal.

'The letter says to put it on, Charlie,' said Mathilda.

He picked it up gingerly. 'It's really cold, and heavy too.'

His head was spinning. It was so strange to almost hear his dad's voice through the pages of the letter and all this talk of being chosen and special was freaking him out. He wasn't special at all. No-one even noticed him at school and he was average at all his subjects. He couldn't even kick a ball straight.

'Here goes,' he said. He lifted the chain carefully over his head and allowed the small stone to settle gently on his chest.

'How do I look?' he asked with a nervous smile.

She was about to reply when the grey stone started to fizz and crackle. He reacted immediately, trying to pull the chain over his head, but it wouldn't move. It seemed like it was glued to his neck. 'It's hot,' he cried, 'it hurts!'

He grimaced in pain as the chain sank slowly into the flesh around his neck. Mathilda tried to pull at it but she couldn't get any purchase on the chain. It was losing its substance as it merged into his skin.

'I can't get it,' she shouted. She scratched and picked at the nearly transparent chain.

'Wait,' said Charlie. 'It's not hurting now, it's...'

The stone glowed brightly on his chest and started to flash intermittently, faster and faster like a strobe light, until finally it vanished.

'Oh my God, Charlie. Your eyes,' said Mathilda in wonder.

The bright blue glow had gone when the stone amulet disappeared, but she could now see it sparkling at the back of his eyes. It was amazing.

'Are you OK, you look, er, different,' she finished weakly.

He felt different too. There was a feeling of surging energy under his skin. It was like something was living within him. He could feel it flowing through him, the tips of his fingers tingled in anticipation of a release of the energy he contained.

'Blimey,' he said with a grin.

'The letter, Charlie, we need to finish it.'

Before you put the amulet on, I should warn you, it will feel a little – strange....

'Thanks, Dad,' he said sarcastically. 'Perhaps I should have read this first.'

Don't be afraid, it is just a part of the process. You're forming a connection with the power in you. Like I said, it's like turning a key in a lock and opening up your powers. For what it's worth I think I was sick when Granddad gave me the stone.

Once it works the stone will become part of you. Only you can remove it. It looks like it's gone but it's still there. If you wanted to you could decide to take it off again. If everything was OK, I wouldn't have passed this on to you until I had been able to teach you everything properly. When I was old and you were ready, then it would have been time to pass the power on to you, the next generation of Watchers. But things have changed and I need to do this now – I can't risk the stone being lost and although I'm weaker without it, I want it to be with you.

'That's what happened,' Charlie exclaimed. 'Dad took off the stone and put it in keeping for me, maybe that's why he was taken. Why didn't he keep it?'

I went away to meet with some of the family. The other Watchers, or at least the ones that were left. We had to try and stop the Nasties, but it was hard, there were so many and they were stronger than ever before. I only just survived, my friends were lost. The Infinite One, the one we call Beleth, will be coming for me – we couldn't finish it. If you have the stone you will be protected. If it comes back, if it comes to find you, you will have a chance and that is all I want, for you to be safe.

I hope you have time to master your power before they return, because I know they will. Even when we have killed them before, somehow they come back. The evil from which they are born is too old and powerful for them to go altogether.

So what next? I'm rambling on, saying lots but telling you nothing.

To business. You have the stone on. It will have done something weird and hopefully you haven't thrown up everywhere. Now I need to try and help you unlock the power it contains. This is going to be hard for me to explain when I'm not actually there with you but I will do my best.

You will feel different, tingly maybe. You might even be able to see the edges of the power flickering in your fingertips. The power will feel very strong – maybe a little frightening. But don't worry. Keep calm, breathe deeply and steadily. Make sure you feel relaxed. Then we will try and get you to do something more interesting. God, I wish I could be with you – this is the best bit.

What I need you to do is summon up a flame into your hands. Believe it or not you have an unlimited store of this energy inside you. It's all yours and you can do what you want with it, you just need to get used to controlling it. Like I said, if you can feel it in your fingertips we are nearly there.

He could feel it. The tips of his fingers felt raw, like they had been out in the cold. As he watched he could see tendrils of light forming, pulsing under his nails. It made him feel vaguely nauseous.

Hold your hands out in front of you, palms up and concentrate – without forcing it, push the power you feel in your fingertips up and out into the palm of your hand. Allow it to flow, don't be afraid, it can't hurt you. It looks like a flame, but it won't burn you. It's your friend – honest!

He breathed deeply and concentrated. He pushed gently with his mind, imagining the energy flowing down his arms and through his fingertips.

Mathilda felt something change in the room. The fine hairs on her arms started to prickle and stand on end. There was a feeling of energy in the air like you got around those big electricity pylons. The fillings in her back teeth ached.

Slowly but surely the light began to build in his hands. The flame rolling gently above his upturned palms, concentrating into a small but dazzlingly bright ball of flame, like a miniature sun.

'What does the letter say now?' cried Charlie. He was unable to take his eyes of the thing he had created. Mathilda hastily picked up the letter from his lap and continued reading in a stammering voice.

The best way, and this is how Granddad explained it to me, is to sort of focus on the gap between your hands. You are trying to pull the power into that space, away from your hands so it floats free.

'Streets ahead of you, Dad,' he cried in a slightly hysterical voice. He was now feeling slightly panicked. The bright blue sun was growing in size. Mathilda watched in fascination.

'What do I do now?' he asked, turning to look at her with a worried look on his face. 'What does the letter say?'

Now – most important – don't panic. What you see can't harm you. I repeat – the energy is yours to control. If you want to you can let it go, but try to direct it away, sort of aim it, otherwise it will just drift off – think of it like throwing something... Mathilda read.

He pulled his hands back towards his chest, seemingly grasping the ball of light which now pulsed between his fingers. It was so bright Mathilda was sure she could almost see the bones in his hands through his skin. With a flick he pushed away. The ball of light flashed past her head through the ceiling and up into the morning sky, leaving a fizzing, crackling energy to dissipate in the room around them.

At the far end of Therwick woods, on the outskirts of town, there was an old manor house. In the shadows of the cellar, the Nasties gathered. Parts of the floor of the house had long since decayed and fallen in, and the sky could be seen through a framework of broken wood and twisted creepers. The local people said this house was haunted. Many years ago it had been a home for a community of people that wanted to live together away from the normal world of jobs, money and all the stress that went with it. They had set up their own farm and grew crops and lived together. But something had gone wrong and a terrible evil had been done. The police had been called after screaming had been heard by a local farmer. The dead bodies and murder they found caused a national scandal. Ever since the house had lain empty. But the feeling of evil remained and this had drawn the Nasties to it. Places like this always did and they made it their home. They now climbed and rolled amongst themselves in the darkened cellar like a pack of unruly wolves, snarling and hissing at each other in the blackness. They had fed recently, but their number was growing by the day and they needed more to eat. The smaller creatures looked to the largest, the Infinite One, who crouched in the shadow cast by the broken floor above. It looked out to the sky and hated what it saw. It hated all of it, from the trees to the clouds and the small animals that scurried away from the house when they sensed what now resided within it. This world and all within it meant nothing. It thought only of feeding. It had seen the blue light cast from the box in the boy's house last night. It wasn't capable of feeling fear as we know it, but when it saw the blue flame flickering within it, it knew that its future on this Earth would not be secure, that an ancient rivalry would soon re-commence.

A flash of blue light suddenly broke into the sky far above the town. It exploded like a firework. The Infinite One bared its fangs and hissed, head writhing back and forth on its powerful shoulders. The smaller Nasties crowded behind it to bare their fangs in unison, clawing outwards at the hated light as it faded slowly away. As ever, an enemy had emerged to challenge them. To stop them feeding. It remained to be seen if it was a strong enough to defeat them, they were growing in number by the day, with new creatures spewed forth from its flesh, born of the energy they had gorged on when they took the girl-child. They would soon be ready.

Charlie looked gingerly at his hands. 'Wow,' said Mathilda softly. 'That was really something.'

'We better finish the letter,' he said.

Practise as much as you can. Perfect your aim and the way you channel the energy.

Now, Charlie, you have to prepare yourself for what is going to come. Once you have unlocked your power, you create a trace in the universe. The Nasties will know you are here and they will ready themselves for battle with you. There is no hiding from that. You can't run away. If you do they will find you anyway. You are Nephilim, a Watcher, and it is your duty to fulfil this role. You might remember I called it a vocation and I could see you didn't really understand what I meant. What I mean is this is what you are meant to do. It is what I did, what your granddad did and what countless other people in our family have done for years and years. You will think it is ridiculous and that all this is crazy, but that won't change anything. The Nasties will still come. It is your job to stop them.

Big stuff for a 7-year-old right? I know, but as I have said there are others like us, people with the same power you have. I have been trying to reach them so they can help you, but no-one has answered me yet. Hopefully by the time you read this someone from the families will already be there with you. They will teach you all you need to know. There is more to it than just the flames, I am learning about other things, new powers that will help us hunt them down, help us track them into the worlds they inhabit outside our own, but I'm not quite there yet – Warragul knows, he can help.

There will also be other people that can see the Nasties. They aren't like us, they aren't Nephilim, they don't have the flame, but they can help. My friend who held this for me is one. I have put his address at the bottom of this letter and you should go to him. There may be other people as well. You never can tell who, but you will know when you meet them.

'That's me, Charlie –he's talking about me.'

He barely heard Mathilda. He was lost in the last words of his missing dad.

For now all I can say is goodbye. I am missing you already as I write this, even though you are upstairs asleep in bed. I wish I could speak to you in person, and hey, maybe I will. Things might work out. Either way, remember that I love you more than anything in the world. And remember that you can do this – we might not look much, but Watchers like me and you, we are the business!

Dad.

He looked away as tears flowed silently down his cheeks. It was agony to read those words. He could see why his mum had been crying last night. He could also see why she hadn't talked about this with him before. It was crazy. She probably thought his dad was a mental case.

'What shall we do now?' Charlie asked in a choked voice.

'We go and see your dad's friend,' she said firmly.

Chapter 5

Peter Bashir, known as Bash to his (admittedly diminishing) circle of friends, was having a nightmare of a morning. His car wouldn't start and his head was aching as a result of one too many drinks in the King's Head last night. He was meant to be working on site this morning. Craig had given him another chance, despite him messing up the week before. He hadn't meant to punch that guy, but he had drunk too many pints at lunchtime and the red mist had descended. He could barely remember why the argument had started, something to do with football, but the outcome was depressingly familiar. A fight, a fall, and a visit to the police cells. He could still remember his life before navigating to his next drink had become his sole ambition but it was getting harder, or maybe it was just getting easier to lose himself in the haze. He had been a businessman once, a man you could rely on and trust. Alex Picker had trusted him, trusted him with the most important thing a man could, his son's life.

If he could think of a moment his life had really started to fall apart, he would probably have to point at the time he met and became friends with Alex Picker. He had been his own boss in those days, running a successful woodcraft and carpentry business, employing five men. Things had been on the up. He had the house, the girlfriend, the expensive car, all that good stuff. The intervening years had been a slow process of removal, erasing one after the other until he was left with this battered old Ford and a house that was falling apart.

Before he'd met Alex, he hadn't believed in anything mystical or strange. He believed in himself, he believed in what he could make with his own hands. His thoughts and his life were as solid as the wood he could skilfully carve and shape. Alex had messed that up. He was like a catalyst. He had opened up his eyes to the other world that existed alongside the world everyone else lived in. He opened his eyes to the Nasties.

Alex had come into his workshop with his then pregnant wife. They had wanted a cot building for their baby, a solid one made out of local oak. Alex had been insistent on that, he said oak was strong and would protect his son. He had built the cot himself and Alex and Cathy were delighted with it. When he delivered it to the large house they lived in on Windmill Hill, he had stayed for a while to drink a glass of beer and celebrate. At that time he could have a few beers, and at least in company he could find the will to stop, to refuse the next glass even when his chest tightened at the thought. In that short time they became friends.

He last saw Alex about a week before he disappeared. He had turned up at his door, looking distracted and troubled. At that point Bash had hoped he wouldn't see him again. The week before they had travelled to some place in the back of nowhere and battled dark things, barely escaping with their lives. Bash had been blind drunk ever since. He had felt a lurch in his stomach when he saw Alex's careful smile as he opened the door. He spelled trouble for him. The things he had seen and done with him over the last few years had sent him over the edge. Fanning the flames of his addiction. No normal person could spend his days killing black-hearted monsters without losing at least a few marbles.

Alex had sat down and explained the Nasties were coming for him. He was scared for Charlie and for himself. Bash had immediately reached for a drink, but Alex hadn't asked him for help in hunting them, instead he had simply handed him a letter and an old chain with a stone hanging from it. He had asked him to promise to send it to Cathy and Charlie if anything happened to him. The booze he was swallowing with indecent speed had already been softening the edges of his anxiety. He had asked where he was planning on going. Alex had smiled sadly, and just asked him to promise to deliver the package. He had shook his hand and hugged him before leaving. A few drinks later he convinced himself that Alex was just winding him up and by the time he fell into bed he was sure he would be back for his package in a week or two.

A week later he had been reading the paper and seen the missing person article, next to a picture of his friend Alex Picker. A month after that he had plucked up the courage to fulfil his promise and delivered the letter and chain to Cathy. He was pretty sure he would have been drunk when he went round there.

She had looked terrible, thin and drawn. Charlie had grown since the last time he had seen him, but he had barely looked up when he said 'Hi.' His eyes remained fixed on the TV screen. Cathy had looked at the letter with a frown that descended swiftly into accusation when she asked him to explain what the hell all this was about. He had told her what happened and about Alex's visit but after ripping open the letter and reading part of it, she had lost it and started screaming at him. He didn't do conflict, not this type anyway, not with someone he liked as much as Cathy. He turned in the face of her fury and ran.

The police had come to his house a few days later, and he told them what he had told Cathy (obviously omitting the bit about monsters). They seemed politely interested but no more than that. They asked if he knew what was in the letter and he said he didn't. They said Cathy had destroyed it and although this clearly annoyed them, as loose ends are always likely to do, reading between the lines even he could see the police had this down as a simple case of a husband running off. They didn't come to see him again. The last time he saw Cathy holding Charlie's hand in town she had crossed the street to avoid him.

He still saw things, dark things in the shadows, but without Alex he couldn't do anything to stop them. So instead he drank to make them disappear and that worked for him.

But monsters weren't on his mind today, just the stupid car that was letting him down. Craig wouldn't give him another chance, he was sure of that. He cursed loudly as he turned the ignition key again and listened to the weak whirr and whine of the engine trying to start. If he had been able to keep up payments on his phone he could have at least called Craig, but his mobile had been dead for weeks.

He looked up the road to see if there was anyone who could help, or offer him a lift, but he knew he was clutching at straws. His neighbours had been studiously ignoring him for years now. He had slowly progressed down the social scale from happy-go-lucky guy who likes a drink and a good time, to the weird drunk fella who jumped at shadows and couldn't be trusted. No-one from around here would be offering him a lift to town.

He rested his forehead against the steering wheel, closing his eyes and breathing deeply through his nose until the anger and frustration in him started to ebb. Maybe a little drink would help, he thought.

Eventually he looked up through the blurred windscreen of the car. There were two kids standing at the end of his drive. His befuddled mind creaked into action. *Who the hell is this?* he thought. *A bunch of kids?* What were they doing here? There were no kids on this road, the school bus that went into town didn't even come this way, it went round to the main part of the village where all the families lived. Maybe they weren't kids, salesmen perhaps, not that he had any cash to buy anything with. He blinked hard. No, it was two kids, one in a green uniform and one in blue, looking at him. Whoever they were, they stood between him and the bottle of whisky he had opened last night.

'Do you think that's him?' whispered Mathilda out of the corner of her mouth.

'This is the address in Dad's letter,' Charlie said. 'I guess it must be.'

He had carefully written that down before they had put the letter in the box and placed it back under the bed. He had been worried. The letter was still there, but the chain and amulet were gone and if his mum looked back in the box he was in trouble. Hopefully she would just put the box back in the loft without checking.

'You said you knew the name, is it him?'

He was starting to wonder if he had written the house number down correctly. He remembered his dad's friend, at least he thought he did. It had been a while ago and people change but it was hard to see that this guy was going to be much use to them. The car he was sitting in looked like it was falling apart, and the house behind it looked little better. He guessed that a while ago it must have been quite nice. It was a big house and Charlie knew some of the richer kids at school lived up here in the village, but it looked like it was a long time since anyone had taken care of this place. Weeds were growing in great thick patches in the cracked paving on the drive, and the glass in the front door was spider-webbed with cracks.

The guy looked ill. His face was pale, even though he had brown skin, and his eyes were sunken deep in his skull. It looked like he was struggling to get out of the car. He did look familiar though – that was something.

As they watched he made another attempt to heave himself out of his seat and stood, weaving ever so slightly on the drive. He rubbed a hand over his face and stared at them.

'What the hell do you want?' he said hoarsely. 'I'm busy, got to get to work. Go away.'

Bash walked unevenly to his front door, where he started to try, with little success, to get the key in the lock. He really wanted that drink now, he could almost taste it.

'My dad said to come and see you. He said you could help me,' said Charlie.

'I don't know your dad,' he replied without looking back. *God, why won't this door open?* he thought. His hands were shaking so badly and not just because he wanted a drink.

Charlie looked at Mathilda desperately. 'My dad is Alex Picker,' he ventured. The man at the door paused, his hand frozen in mid turn. Slowly he leaned forward and rested his head and then both his hands against the door, the key left swaying gently in the lock. He stayed that way for a while.

'I said my dad is Alex...'

'I heard what you said,' the man replied. 'They're back aren't they?' he said in a flat monotone. 'I knew they would be, one day at least.' He sighed heavily. 'If you're looking for help you've come to the wrong place. I'm no help to anyone.........can't even help myself.'

He quickly turned the key and opened the door. He went inside without another word. The door hung open and shortly after they heard the soft clink of a bottle rattling against a glass.

'Can we at least talk to you?' called Mathilda. 'We don't know what to do.' She looked at Charlie nervously and together they walked through the open door.

The house was, predictably, a mess. There were empty bottles everywhere and a faint smell of cigarette smoke and fried bacon. The windows were dirty and the inside of the house existed in a permanent twilight. The heavy carpet was soiled and felt sticky under their feet. When Charlie flicked on the light switch nothing happened.

They headed forward into the front room. The man was now sitting in an armchair facing a dead TV screen. They could see the top of his head and an arm hanging to one side. In the hand was a large glass of what looked like dirty water. The man tipped his head back and drained the glass in one massive gulp.

'You look like him, you know,' he said. 'You have the same eyes, very blue.' He took another gulp of his drink. 'I've not been that welcome down your neck of the woods. It's been a while since I last saw you. You've grown.'

He turned in his chair and looked at Mathilda with bleary eyes. 'And where do you fit in?' he asked.

'I'm Mathilda, a friend of Charlie's. I—I can see the things too, the Nasties that is,' she whispered. 'At least I can now, I didn't before but then the other week it just...well it just...' She couldn't finish, she didn't have the words to explain.

He looked at her with something like sympathy in his eyes, before barking out a short bitter laugh.

'You poor thing. History has a habit of repeating itself, well, welcome to hell,' he finished with a flourish, before attempting to swig back his now empty glass. He looked at it with annoyance, sweeping his other hand along the side of his chair, looking for the bottle of whisky.

Mathilda could feel herself getting angry. The man was a drunk. It was obvious he knew something about what was going on, but if he carried on knocking back drinks like that he wasn't going to be capable of doing anything. The sharp smell of whisky filled the room as they watched him splosh another large measure into his glass. He stared at it with owl-like concentration as he poured, blinking slowly. When he spoke again his voice was thicker and he slurred slightly.

'Sorry, kids, I'm not what you are looking for. I'm busy at the moment – no time to spare.' He peered into the glass as he spoke, hesitating ever so slightly before throwing back his head and downing the precious, restorative liquid. He closed his eyes.

'They've taken a little girl,' said Mathilda. 'Don't you understand, we see them all the time. There are more and more of them. We think they are starting to feed. Charlie's dad said you would be able to help,' she finished desperately.

Bash didn't move in his chair. With his eyes closed he filled his glass again, this time spilling some, unnoticed, onto his lap. He said nothing.

'This is pointless, Charlie,' said Mathilda. 'Let's go, we'll have to deal with this ourselves.' She turned stiffly and started to walk out of the room. Charlie looked on helplessly at the back of Bash's head.

'Please, Mr Bashir, we're lost. This letter from Dad, it said you could help. That you would look after me. Please...'His voice tailed off weakly. Mathilda grabbed his arm and pulled him gently from the room.

Bash heard the front door slam shut. He opened his eyes and stared carefully at his distorted reflection in the blank TV screen. The glass in his hand was empty. It always was these days, one way or another, he thought. The whisky had softened his panic but the feeling of terror he associated with those dark days with Alex was there, buried, but not deep enough. How could they know if those things were back? he reasoned. They were just kids, even if Charlie was Alex's son. He couldn't do it. He had done enough. It was not his fight anymore. He allowed the whisky to envelop him. Eyes closed, he drifted into unconsciousness.

When he awoke it was darker in the room, the daylight had swung round to the back of the house. He felt sick. Disorientated and on unsteady legs he weaved across the room to the door and out into the hall. *God, how long have I been out for?* he wondered. He blacked out so quickly these days when he hit the whisky hard. His mouth tasted sour and metallic as he leaned unsteadily against the door frame.

He couldn't hear anyone outside. He peered down the hall through the broken glass in the front door. There didn't seem to be anyone there. *They must have gone, thank God,* he thought. He looked back down the hall towards the kitchen. He knew where he had put it, locked away somewhere safe. Steadying himself against the wall, he dropped to his knees and began pulling boxes and rubbish out from the under stairs cupboard. It was there, at the back, wrapped in an old blanket. His heart was beating loudly in his chest, as he held the precious bundle tightly in his hands. Its weight was reassuring and although his hands were shaking, it felt good to hold it again. He returned to his chair and carefully unwrapped the bundle.

He looked down at the axe now resting across his knees. Its blade was still razor sharp, as any good woodman's axe should be, he thought with a small smile. Its edge shimmered slightly in the darkness. Without thinking he poured the remainder of the whisky into his glass and tossed the empty bottle to one side where it spun to a slow stop on the grubby carpet. As he raised the glass to his lips, the blade of the axe ignited a sudden and brilliant blue. The magic was still there, he marvelled, the drink for once forgotten in his hand.

Chapter 6

Simon Crenshaw pulled the saddle and tack down from the hook by the stable door and heaved it over his shoulder. It was a beautiful evening and his mum had said he could take his pony out for ride along the bridleway that ran all the way from his parents' farm to the village. He loved his pony. It had been his sister's until she had grown too big for him, but now Sweep was his. He was a short, stocky Welsh hill pony, never destined to win any beauty contests, but he had character, at least that's what his dad said. He was certainly stubborn, thought Simon as he carefully got into Sweep's stable. If it was raining or even a bit windy you had no chance of getting the saddle on him. But he had no problem today. Sweep was very obliging, and in a short time he was pulling on his old jacket and encouraging Sweep to get them underway. His mum was out in the yard and he waved to her as they sauntered towards the gate and the field beyond. 'Remember to keep to the bridleway,' she called. 'And be back by six-thirty for tea.' He waved over his shoulder in acknowledgment.

She was always slightly nervous letting him out on his own, he was only twelve and small for his age, but Pete said it would be good for his confidence and besides it wasn't that far to the village. She looked at the portly shape of the pony as he carried Simon slowly through the thick meadow grass. Sweep wasn't going to win any races, not unless there was a particularly big bag of oats waiting for him, but he was a good old thing and she was sure he would look after him.

The bridleway ran the full length of the meadow alongside the farm, before plunging into a small copse of trees that led to the woods and the village beyond. If Sweep was moving at top speed (a leisurely plod) Simon would expect to be at the village in about thirty minutes and back in maybe a little longer. Sweep always stopped for refreshments on the way back, and you couldn't get him to move until he was done. It was part of his charm. He enjoyed the evening sun on his face as they turned onto the path and made their way carefully towards the old oak tree that marked the start of the copse. The path was muddy and churned up as a result of heavy rain the night before, but Sweep plodded on, oblivious. Dad always said Welsh ponies were tough, they were used to much worse weather in the mountains from which they originated. Simon couldn't imagine Sweep standing much discomfort these days. He liked his warm stable and his hay. He had earned his comfortable retirement.

It was only when they entered the wood, that he noticed just how still it was this evening. And quiet too. He usually heard the mad cackle of a magpie or a jay and the steady trill of various warblers and songbirds, but the wood was silent. It was cooler under the trees and the smell of the damp soil was stronger. As they approached the denser trees that bracketed the pathway to the village, he felt Sweep begin to pick up the pace slightly. By the time they had reached the corner where the path split in two he was cantering and that was practically unheard off. Simon could hear the little pony's breathing, rasping out between the bit in his teeth. He pulled back gently on his reins to bring him to halt. 'Steady on, you silly old thing,' he said affectionately, patting Sweep's heaving flank. He looked to his left, down the path that led to the old manor house. He didn't want to go that way. On that he agreed with his mum and dad. It was a place best avoided. It looked so dark down there, he thought, even though the trees were no thicker. Sweep trembled under him, wheezing after his efforts. Concerned, he swung his leg over and jumped down to the floor. The old thing was terrified, he thought as he tried to reassure it, pushing his face onto Sweep's soft muzzle and blowing gently.

The Nasties had felt the presence of the boy before they even smelled him. He cast a ripple in the air that was picked up by their finely tuned senses. As one they salivated, growling in the darkness of the cellar, leaping nimbly over each other as they headed up towards the evening light. The Infinite One, known as Beleth to the Watchers, took the lead, moving slickly up and over the edge of the broken floor before scrambling up into the branches of the nearest tree. It hung from the thickest limb, stretching out sightlessly like a huge leech as it sniffed the still evening air. A mouth cracked open, revealing layer after layer of razor-sharp teeth. It howled in savage joy and swung quickly away, up into the canopy of the trees. The other Nasties scrambled out of the cellar to follow.

Simon was starting to worry. Sweep wouldn't move despite him pulling on the reins. He was stubborn, but this was different. The old pony's eyes were rolling in his head. He seemed to be staring down the path towards the house and it was starting to freak him out. 'Come on, Sweep, we need to go...' he pleaded. Fear radiated off the pony. It was infectious, Simon could feel his own stomach churning and the hairs on the back of his neck prickled. He looked over his shoulder down the path. There was something moving in the trees. The evening was still but the branches were rustling wildly and he heard the sound of one breaking further away, a sharp crack like a pistol shot that made him jump.

Beleth could see the boy. He was standing next to the animal, staring up into the tree where it crouched. He couldn't see them yet, but he would soon. They always did when the time came, but by then it would be too late. Beleth felt its kin gathering around it, and with a fluid push, flew out and across the path, landing with cat-like dexterity just down the path from the boy.

Simon felt rather than saw Beleth land. A thick smell of corruption smothered him. He covered his nose and mouth with one hand as he stumbled back against Sweep's flank. A black shape seemed to twist up from the ground and form in front of him. Sweep reared up, whinnying wildly, and before he had time to think the pony was off, dragging him along next to him, his legs flying across the ground in exaggerated strides. He managed to throw his arms and then his leg over Sweep's back and set himself in the saddle. Sweep's head bobbed up and down frantically as he raced back up the path towards his home. Out of the corner of his eye Simon saw something large and black racing alongside them.

Beleth screamed in anger as the stupid beast dragged his prize away. Its stride elongated, smoothly accelerating until it was just behind the pony's hooves. The boy was crouched low over his back, but the pony was slowing. He was old and weak. Beleth carefully stretched out a claw-like hand, which flicked nonchalantly at Sweep's trailing leg. With terrible inevitability the little pony stumbled and fell hard into the muddy ground, his face pushing a heavy furrow into the muck as he slid to a halt. The boy flew over his head and thumped against a tree, landing in the thick layer of old leaves that carpeted the floor. Beleth skidded to a halt, pausing briefly to sniff the body of the pony that now lay very still on the floor. He was dead.

Simon wasn't dead, but he was unconscious, which was probably just as well. The Nasties gathered around him in the now silent wood. In turn they each howled up at the sky, teeth bared and viciously happy. Beleth reached down and picked up his slumped body, slits opening in its face, inhaling deeply. It enveloped him in its blackness and with a blur of movement the Nasties swirled up into the air as one, through the treetops like a rolling black smoke before plunging down into the cellar of the house.

Chapter 7

The man who was sitting on the makeshift bench in front of the porta-cabin looked sick. Even from a distance Craig could see he was shivering despite it being a warm day. It was only when the man looked up briefly that he recognised him. *Bloody hell*, he thought. *Is that Bash?*

He had never been able to understand how a man could get himself into such a state with drink. Nor had he ever met anyone with the capacity for self-destruction that Bash seemed to have. Craig took a deep breath and carried on walking towards his office; he liked Bash but this couldn't go on any longer. He was getting it in the neck every time he didn't turn up on site (and in truth even when he did turn up). The trouble was there were very few carpenters that were as talented as him, and on the special bespoke projects Craig did, he knew it would be impossible to replace him. He braced himself as he stopped in front of Bash, who sat with his head in his hands.

Before he could speak Bash looked up at him, squinting slightly. To his surprise Bash's eyes were clear, if a little bloodshot. He had also expected to smell the booze on him. You could usually catch a whiff of Bash before he was within ten feet of you. But not today. He looked different and it took him a few moments before he realised why. Pete Bashir was sober.

Bash had heard about the missing boy a week after his visit from Charlie and Mathilda. Another missing child, in the woods this time, the paper had said. The article mentioned the missing little girl as well, her toothy grin in evidence on the picture that ran alongside the headline. That was two gone inside two weeks. The police had noticed some similarities in the disappearances but in truth you could read between the lines of the police inspector's carefully prepared statements. They were baffled – it seemed like both of them had vanished into thin air. From experience he knew that was probably not that far from the truth.

It had been seven days since he had last had a drink, and although his body cried out for it, his head was now clear, clearer than it had been in a very long time. This clarity had its downside. The memories were coming back, so strong and unpleasant that more than anything he just wanted to drink himself into silent oblivion. But he couldn't. Not yet at least. He had to find

Charlie and the girl. He knew that he had a role to play in this next chapter of the war (as Alex had been fond of calling it after a few beers). He also knew that Charlie would need his help.

Alex had always said the flame would pass to his son, but he knew from the stories he had told him that his own dad had spent many months, years even, helping Alex understand what he could do and how to do it. Charlie had been denied that luxury, but he thought he could remember a few of the tricks they had used in the old days. He also needed him to light up his axe again. The blue glow that told him there was still a job for him to do was fading, but he thought he could show Charlie what to do on that front – Alex had passed the flame to him enough times and he remembered how he did it. Then they would have to go hunting.

Craig was left feeling a little bemused and more than a bit ashamed. Bash had come into his office and apologised for all the trouble he had caused him. He had said he had some stuff to do over the next few weeks and so wouldn't be able to help him finish the job. Craig had breathed a sigh of relief and counted his blessings that a difficult conversation had been avoided. When he left he shook the hand Bash offered him and wished him well. He was not sure why but he couldn't shake the feeling that he wouldn't be seeing Pete Bashir again.

A police car turned slowly up Church Street, towards the school. The chief inspector had requested that the two available patrol vehicles were highly visible in and around the parts of Therwick where children were regularly seen. This, he had said at the morning briefing, created the right perception in the eyes of the public of a focused and dedicated police operation. *It also helps hide the fact that we don't have a clue where those two children have gone*, thought Police Constable Carl Duckworth as he swung the car onto the hill that led up to the secondary school.

Carl had been on shift for days. The town's police force was small and the recent turn of events meant they were dangerously overstretched and pretty exhausted. More officers had been drafted in from the larger surrounding towns, but Carl and his colleagues wanted to find the missing children themselves. As a result he hadn't slept properly for three days. They had had to send Mike Tavers home when he had fallen asleep at his desk.

The disappearance of Simon had upped the ante, hence the very public appearance of the chief inspector, Hudson he was called, who up until last week he had never even seen, never mind met. The message to the schools and parents was clear. Be vigilant, keep an eye on your kids, where possible avoid secluded places, and make sure they walk home with an adult or in groups.

It had occurred to him that Lottie had been in her back garden when she vanished, so perhaps avoiding secluded places wasn't going to be enough, but messages like that weren't going to help calm down an already unsettled community. There was quite a bit about the two disappearances that bothered the team at the station.

The dead horse and the violently churned ground in the woods suggested a terrible struggle had taken place, but the forensics team had come up with exactly nothing. The same applied to Lottie Peacock. The only sign she had ever been in the garden that afternoon was her discarded rag doll, and that wasn't giving anything away.

He felt so bad for the parents. Simon was at the same school as his own daughter and the thought that someone could take a child, in his town, was driving him crazy. What if it had been his own daughter that had been snatched? The idea made him feel physically sick, his hands tightening on the steering wheel.

He had never been involved in anything like this before. Dealing with local drunks and junkies, the odd car accident, had been the extent of his policing up until now. Sometimes he had wished things could be more exciting, but not like this. Not seeing hope fading in the faces of Lottie and Simon's parents as each day passed.

They all knew that timing was critical if they were to find them. The longer they remained missing the less chance of finding them alive, however many laps of the town they had to do in the squad cars.

Bash walked up the footpath towards the secondary school. The last thing he wanted was to be seen lurking around a school but he needed to find Mathilda. He had been to Charlie's school the day before, carefully putting on his best and cleanest clothes so he looked less conspicuous, but he hadn't been able to speak with him. He had seen him in a small group of children being led out of the gates by a rather large and unpleasant looking woman. She reminded him of a strutting hen as she led them away, smiling and nodding at some of the parents that had gathered at the school to collect their kids. He noticed how that smile had swiftly faded once the parents were gone. He didn't fancy speaking with her.

He had seen in the local paper that schools were arranging for some kids to be accompanied home if there was no-one to collect them. The town had hunkered down, siege-like, after the boy had gone missing. He decided Charlie would have to wait. He couldn't go to his house. There was no way Cathy would want to speak to him. He wasn't ready for that conversation yet.

Besides, he hadn't even seen a Nastie himself and he clung to the hope that they were wrong, and the kids were just missing or, if the worst had happened, it was a normal (if that was the right word) nutter that had abducted them.

He didn't know what time school finished these days but figured that it he got there around about two-thirty he wouldn't be far wrong.

He walked slowly up the hill with an old newspaper tucked under his arm. When he saw the police car heading his way, his heart had sank. He was known to the police, albeit as a drunk and a troublemaker, but he knew that if they saw him they would want to ask him what he was doing, and given he had a large axe stowed in the inside of his coat he was painfully aware that such discussions could get quite difficult for him.

He cursed inwardly at his stupidity for bringing it with him, but its soft blue glow made him feel safe.

He heard the sound of the car engine swelling behind him as it accelerated slightly up the hill. He dropped casually to his knee and pretended to do up his laces. He held his head low and turned his face slightly away from the road just in case, breathing a sigh of relief as the police car moved steadily up the hill past the school before indicating left down onto the estate that backed onto the school playing field.

He continued to the school gate, where a small number of parents had already gathered, chatting to each other in small groups. One or two eyed him suspiciously as he walked past them. He tried to look natural as he stopped to wait a bit further on. He imagined what a father would look like standing there waiting, with nothing to hide, and so he whistled softly to himself whilst looking out over the playing field. There were some kids doing something.

They looked like some of the older ones, he guessed, given they were shooting bows and arrows. He didn't remember doing that at school, they were lucky if they got a ball to kick around. Things changed, he thought. He noticed there was a girl off to the side on her own. She seemed to have a bigger bow than the rest of them and her target was much further away. He watched with interest as she fired a series of arrows in quick succession into the target. A guy in a tracksuit applauded enthusiastically as she walked across to retrieve them. As she did so she pushed her hair up and out of her face, and he realised who he was seeing. It was the girl from the other week, Charlie's friend. Mathilda. He looked at the arrows sticking directly out of the centre of the target in a neat cluster. He noticed the confident way she pulled them free and placed them over her shoulder back into her quiver.

He smiled. She was a hunter as well.

Mrs. Whelan didn't recognize the man standing to the far left of the school gate. He looked uncomfortable and kept looking up and down the road as if he was expecting someone to pick him up. His skin was brown but he looked pale and slightly sweaty, despite the relatively cool afternoon. She had been told to report any suspicious activity or people to Mr. Ward. He had been very clear on that point when the group of volunteer playground monitors had been briefed a week or so ago shortly after Simon had disappeared.

Mrs Whelan was just about to seek him out (he was busy shepherding the year sevens to the front gate, where their parents waited in various stages of agitation) when one of the year tens walked slowly up to the man and they started to talk. She couldn't remember her name, although she prided herself on having a nodding acquaintance with all the children at the school—was it Megan, she thought? They looked like they knew each other and she was swiftly distracted by a tug on her sleeve from another anxious parent who hadn't been able to find her daughter. By the time she looked again both the girl and the man were gone.

'So why are you here then?' asked Mathilda as they walked down the street towards town.

Bash walked with his head hung low. He could understand why she wasn't pleased to see him after his last performance, but he wanted to put things right. He wanted to stop thinking about the little boy who had been taken since they spoke. The words he needed wouldn't come, and he wrestled desperately for them as they approached the high street. He could sense the exasperation coming off her in waves. It reminded him of those last few months with his girlfriend, before she had walked out on him, when everything he did or said was wrong.

'I—I just wanted to make sure Charlie was OK.' Bash paused, searching for the words, his voice hoarse. 'I heard about what happened to the boy and I wanted to help.'

Mathilda was in turn elated and annoyed. Elated because she desperately wanted someone, a grown-up, to help. Annoyed because it had to be this man, who looked like he may have more problems than solutions. It had also taken him far too long to come good for them.

It had been horrible when Simon was taken. Neither she nor Charlie had known what to do. They knew what was responsible, but were powerless to do anything.

Charlie was getting better and better at creating the blue flames but he didn't know what to do with them. They were useless without some guidance. The Nasties had continued to keep clear of them. Charlie thought they were watching him, but he couldn't get sight of one. It was like they were assessing him, before they decided what to do next. It was a standoff but it felt like all the odds were in the Nasties' favour. Having Bash here with her made it feel like the balance was starting to shift ever so slightly towards them, even if he didn't look like a conventional hero in his crumpled suit and dirty work boots.

'Let's go and see if we can catch up with Charlie. He's part of a group of children that get walked home. A lady who runs our counselling group volunteered. I should be able to convince her that he can walk with me.' She paused, looking at Bash. 'Err, you better stay out of sight.'

Esther was annoyed. She couldn't hide it from the group of children waiting patiently in the car park of the school (nor did she want to really). She did have to maintain a pleasant and smiling appearance for the parents and teachers who moved in and around the school gates, and that was a bit more difficult. Her large doughy face was struggling to conceal her feelings. She was trying to remember why she had volunteered for this in the first place.

It had seemed like a good idea at the time. A good chance to show Mrs. McGildrey what a great team player she was. She hadn't realised how many of these kids would actually need escorting home. So many parents who left their kids to their own devices, and now it was people like her who had to make sure they were seen safely home. It was no wonder they all needed counselling. If they really cared for them they would come and get them themselves, she thought angrily. She noticed Charlie Picker dragging his feet down the path towards them.

She reviewed her clipboard with a deliberate and over-exaggerated casualness, before trilling across to him, 'Hurry up, Charlie, yes you, Charlie Picker, we're waiting for you.'

Charlie couldn't believe his bad luck when he was assigned to Esther's group. Of all the people it would have to be her. He was with four other children who lived in roughly the same part of town as he did.

Some of the other 'collectors' had agreed to drive their groups home, but Esther had insisted that they walk together instead. The exercise would be good for them, she said.

Walking was not a problem, most of them would have done that anyway. It was walking with her that made it horrible. He couldn't understand why Esther spent so much time with children, when it was so obvious she couldn't stand them. He was not convinced they were any safer with her than with a Nastie.

'There we are, Charlie, I thought you would have realised we need to set off promptly by now,' said Esther. She pushed into him slightly with her elbow as she brushed past him. 'Let's get a move on, I have better things to do this evening than plod around town with you lot.' With a sigh he trailed behind her, hefting his school bag onto his shoulder. At least it wasn't too far.

Mathilda and Bash arrived just too late to catch Charlie. The car park was emptying, with just a few children milling about waiting to be collected. A teacher, who Mathilda thought she recognized, stood with them.

'Where is he?' she exclaimed. 'They must have set off, we need to catch up with him.' For some reason she was feeling increasingly anxious. She could feel her heart rate picking up and butterflies in her stomach.

'Easy, Mathilda,' replied Bash. 'I'm sure he hasn't gone far – which way would he go? Up there?'

She nodded, pointing in the direction of a path. 'Hey, try to relax,' he said as she edged past him and started to move quickly ahead. He had to walk fast to catch her up, his pace increasing when Mathilda started to jog, her hair swinging from side to side.

'Mathilda, wait, slow down for goodness sake,' he gasped.

She was nearly running now and would have disappeared from view if Bash hadn't started doing the same. It had been a long time since he had done this much exercise and before too long he was wheezing and slipping in the oily mud. The feeling of anxiety was contagious. He was starting to sense something was very wrong. There was a stillness in the air despite the fresh breeze that softly rustled the leaves in the treetops above him. No bird song, no sounds at all. Something was going to happen, he could feel it.

The Beleth saw the woman that led the procession of children up the narrow path. She smelled like the old house, empty and devoid of goodness. Over the years they had encountered humans like her, they were always useful. You could rely on them to do nothing, to look the other way, see nothing, and say nothing. Occasionally the more susceptible would do things for them. Everyone had a price, but for ones like this, it was often very low.

The Beleth had been keeping clear of the boy since the blue fire had burst across the sky. The last child they had taken was gone now, they had used up what food he provided and left his shell in the cellar along where he slowly disintegrated. What remained would never be identified. They didn't waste anything. They needed to feed again and it also felt the irresistible urge to get rid of the boy with the blue flame.

It looked down on the group of children walking away up the tree-lined path that bordered the park. The woman was now behind them waving her arms impatiently. At the front of them walked the boy with the flame. The Nasties gathered around the Beleth, a broiling mass of black that moved and shifted like a nest of snakes. The need for food was overpowering. It was sure that the boy wasn't ready to fight. Just having flames meant nothing, there was more to being a Watcher (as they so piteously described themselves) than simple possession. You had to know what to do with it as well. Aching hunger spurred them on, creating a momentum that would not be denied. One by one they spiralled up and into the air, speeding ahead of the children into the thick treetops.

Charlie walked as far away from Esther as possible. He could hear her tutting and moaning behind him. At least his house was first on the route, he thought. He could shut the door on this and forget about everything for a while, maybe practise producing the flames a bit. He thought he was getting pretty good at it.

Ahead of him the Nasties descended.

Three of them landed in front of him. He stopped suddenly, and the boy behind him, Lewis, walked into his back. 'Watch out, Charlie,' he cried. Esther's voice carried over to him. 'Get a move on, Charlie,' she shouted. 'What on earth are you waiting for?'

On the path ahead of him the Nasties crouched. They had picked the spot for the attack well. The path was at its narrowest, and although Charlie knew the park and its open spaces was over to his right, the old fence panels blocked his escape. He could see tantalising glimpses of green grass through the rotten slats. He heard the protests of Lewis and the other children behind him before he was pushed to one side as Esther moved past him, muttering under her breath. Her hand grabbed hard on his shoulder as she spun him round to face her. Her angry face crowded in front of him, her finger jabbing him in the chest.

'What are you doing, Charlie Picker?'

Each word was punctuated by a fresh prod from her pudgy finger. He barely noticed her, his eyes fixed on the Nasties. They moved steadily up the path towards him, grinning insanely. He could smell their hunger, saw how the saliva running from their open mouths fizzled and smoked when it hit the floor. They weren't the biggest, certainly not like the thing that had splatted against the school window, but they were big enough. They had come, just like his dad said they would. He didn't know what to do. The flames and the feeling of power he associated with it had gone, shrunk away deep down inside him, like a whipped dog.

Esther continued to push and shout at him, noises he barely heard. He sensed something change in the appearance of the Nasties. It was almost like a ripple passed through them. They became somehow more solid, more there. The Nasties were revealing themselves.

As if on cue Esther looked down the path, her finger stopping in mid prod. Her mouth fell open, a soft whine escaping her lips. Without pausing she pushed him roughly towards the Nasties, moving quickly back up the path, barging the other three children to one side. They had been trying to peek around Esther, to see what was going on. Lewis looked straight into the blood-red eyes of the nearest grinning Nastie and screamed.

The shrill scream echoed down the path. Despite his breathlessness, Bash found the energy to run faster, his hand stealing inside his coat to the handle of his axe.

He could see Mathilda ahead of him. He was gaining on her. Up ahead he could see a group of children shouting and trying to run back towards them. A large woman had got hold of one of the children, a small girl wriggling under her arm as she backed away. A boy lay on the floor, pitched up on his elbows, scrambling his legs back and forth as he tried to get to his feet.

'Charlie,' shouted Mathilda. Hearing his name he looked back over his shoulder, his eyes wide and terrified. In front of him loomed a dark and terrible shape. Bash's stomach lurched. A Nastie – after all this time.

The Nastie closest to Charlie squatted, its haunches quivering as it readied itself to attack. The two behind it were similarly poised. It saw Bash and bared its fangs, a cavernous mouth opening, like a slash ripped across its head. Its teeth were long, thin and needle sharp. *So many teeth*, Bash thought incoherently as he pulled the axe out from the lining of his coat. The blade glowed a faint blue, but flickered slightly, stuttering like a defective bulb. 'Please God let it work,' he muttered to himself, as he swung it over his shoulder. *And let my aim be as good as it used to be*, he prayed as he released it.

The axe whistled through the air, the blade turning over on itself in a blur of blue. It landed with a meaty crunch in the centre of the Nastie's head, splitting it nearly in two. The blue light emanating from the blade flashed brighter still, strobing rapidly before the light was eclipsed by a splat of thick dark blood as the Nastie's head exploded. The blood sprayed across Charlie's face and body as he pulled himself up and started to run back to where Bash and Mathilda now stood. He barely looked at Esther who remained rooted to the spot, holding the little girl in front of her. The Nastie howled, its dying screams echoed by the two that remained. The axe fell from the broken skull of the Nastie's, whose form was flickering in and out of view as it lost substance, its magic spent.

'Charlie, get behind me. You, lady, get over here,' shouted Bash.

Lewis and the other child got safely behind Mathilda. Esther wouldn't move. Her eyes were flat and dead, as if she was in a trance. She slowly lifted the little girl up in front of herself, like an offering. The remaining Nasties started to move cautiously towards her, pausing to sniff at the axe that lay on the path. It was just an old wood axe now. It could do nothing to hurt them.

The Beleth watched the scene unfold from the top of the trees by the path. It had seen the old man with his weapon and felt keenly the death of its spawn. The arrival of this old fool was unexpected, and anger and hatred boiled inside it. It had been wise to wait and see what power they had. It could always sacrifice a few of its brothers to test the readiness of enemies. Now wasn't the time, but they needed to feed, if nothing else they needed to replace those that were lost. It screamed its wishes to the two below, before spiralling up and away into the gaps between the worlds, back to the sanctuary of the old cellar.

The two Nasties paused, their eyes flickering between the groups of humans on the path. The hunger was on them. They stared balefully at the empty woman who offered them food. The old man, the killer, was too far away to stop them, besides, he no longer had a weapon. He was just like the rest. Powerless.

The boy with the flame, the Nasties could sense it dancing beneath his skin, was frozen in terror. He wouldn't do anything either, but those flames meant he would have to wait. They wanted to avenge the death of their brother, but for today this child that was offered to them would be enough.

Bash saw what was happening. The Nasties turned away and focused their attention on the woman and the wriggling girl that was proffered before her. Without thinking he ran towards them, leaping forward, unaware he was screaming at the woman to run, to let the child go. The Nasties roared, stretching claws impossibly forward. They snatched the screaming little girl. Esther, smiling faintly, relinquished her grip and promptly fainted. Bash's trailing leg caught her bulk and he fell to one side, his outstretched hand missing the hem of the girl's school skirt by a fraction. The Nasties screamed in pleasure before enveloping the child in blackness and spiralling up and away. Both Lewis and the other little boy were both in a dead faint.

Bash pushed himself up off the floor. He stared down at his hands. So close to saving the girl, he thought, but not close enough. He turned and looked at Mathilda and Charlie who stood ashen-faced behind him.

'Where have they taken her?' he asked, almost to himself. 'There's still time – if we get to her quickly we might be able to save her, we might...' he said, his voice cracking with despair, his eyes wide and desperate. Slowly he came back to himself, his face hardened. 'That woman, she let them take her, what type of person would do that?'

Mathilda picked up his axe, brushing the mud off its blade before handing it to him. 'You need to get out of here,' she said. She pointed at Esther's slumped body. 'When she wakes up, there's going to be hell to pay. We need to call the police and we can't explain what you were doing here.'

'We can't explain anything,' said Charlie in a strangled sob. 'I, I froze. I'm sorry I didn't know what to do.' He stared at them helplessly. 'Fat lot of use I am.'

Bash put his hands on Charlie's shoulders and knelt down in front of him. 'Charlie,' he said, gently pushing his knuckle under his chin to encourage him to look at him. 'Don't blame yourself, there was nothing you could have done. It's my fault, I should have been here sooner. For you, for them. I won't let you down again. I can help you, I will be in touch very soon, look after each other. No messing about, this is no game.'

Esther stirred on the floor, moaning softly.

'You need to go, Bash,' repeated Mathilda more urgently. 'Now.'

Bash ruffled Charlie's hair and moved off quickly down the path, before cutting in across the side of the park. He stole a glance over his shoulder and saw Mathilda putting her arm over Charlie's shoulder who stood stiffly, his head hung low. The park was mercifully empty and Bash moved quickly along the edge until he reached the gate that took him back towards town.

Chapter 8

Police Constable Carl Duckworth was at a loss. The woman, Esther
Carrington the school counsellor, was no use to them. From what they could
determine she had sustained no injuries, but she was in a near catatonic
state. The doctors said she might come out of it soon, but then again she
might not. Her reaction was consistent with extreme trauma and it affected
people in different ways. He would just have to wait. The children were no
better. No-one could remember anything past leaving the school and heading
up the path towards Albert Road. The older girl, he hadn't seen her statement
yet, but he understood she had only seen Esther on the floor and the children
in various states of hysteria when she had arrived on scene. Either way
another child was gone, this time in broad daylight and still no witnesses.

The boy, Charlie, was understandably distraught and could add little beyond
his anguish at not being able to help. God, he was only ten, even if he was
quite a big lad, thought Carl, what could he have done? He stared into the
bottom of his plastic coffee cup. Whoever had taken Lottie, Simon and now
Sophie was clearly an extremely dangerous character. The media had
descended on the town en masse. Therwick was headline news and the ability
of the police force to deal with the situation was being called into question.

Chief Inspector Hudson had visibly aged, the grey hair around his temples
and thick lines in his face stark in the harsh light of the press room. Carl felt
about ten years older himself. There was talk of closing down the schools (or
at least the primary schools) whilst they drafted in more police to help find
whoever was doing these terrible things. He closed his eyes and allowed his
head to rock back. It was after midnight and the canteen at the station was
quiet, just a few officers milling around over by the coffee machine, talking in
low voices. Carl didn't recognise any of them, there were lots of new faces.
The local police had been pushed to the fringes of the investigation. He had
been lucky to even sit in on the interview with Esther.

He turned his attention to the large window that looked out over the station
car park. He could see the vans from the TV companies parked tightly against
the wall. Reporters milled back and forth under the harsh glow of the security

lights, waiting for developments. What developments? he thought, it was like they had vanished into thin air.

Cathy Picker nearly slammed the door in Bash's face. She would have done if he hadn't quickly put his boot in the way. The door bounced back off his toe with a shudder and he hopped back from the doorstep wincing.

'What are you doing here, Pete?' she asked angrily. Bash recovered his composure, fighting an overwhelming urge to massage his foot.

'Cath, I need to speak with Charlie, I need to speak with both of you.'

She narrowed her eyes. Bash looked better than he did the last time she had seen him weaving up the high street, drunk as a lord. They had been such good friends, but him turning up with that stupid letter, full of stuff that made no sense, stuff that would only encourage Charlie to get involved in the crazy world that Alex had gone on about. She didn't want to go there now, any more than she did when she tore the letter to pieces in the weeks that followed Alex going missing.

'Please, Cath, this is serious, Charlie's in danger. I need to help him,' he pleaded.

Her stomach lurched. 'What are you getting him involved in, Pete? Do you have any idea what type of week we've had? Do you even read the news, or are you still too busy getting drunk? He was nearly abducted, by whatever lunatic is stalking around Therwick. So if you've got something to say about that I suggest you go to the police.' She pushed the door shut, moving her weight against it as Bash wedged himself between the frame again.

'Please, Cath,' he cried. 'It's connected to Alex. The police can't help us.'

Her eyes widened in anger. 'Right, that's it. No, not that rubbish again. He's only a little boy, if you want to go off chasing your imaginary monsters leave him out of it.' She struggled against the door. 'Seriously, Pete, if you don't go, I'm going to call the police.'

'Mum?' called Charlie as he came down the stairs from his room. 'Who's that?'

He had heard the commotion and wanted to see what was going on. He could see his mum pushing furiously at the front door, and the startled face of Bash as he tried to edge his way into the porch. 'Mum,' he called again, louder this time. 'Wait, Mum, let him in – he's, he's my friend.'

Cathy looked back over her shoulder in despair. 'Go back to your room, Charlie, this is nothing to do with you.'

'Cathy, for God's sake,' Bash said in a strangled voice, his head now wedged between the door and the frame. 'Charlie needs my help, all that stuff Alex said to you was true, it's all real, please...'

'Mum, let him in, I do need his help,' said Charlie. 'The Nasties are everywhere. The children that are missing, they were taken by them. I don't know what Dad ever said to you about this, but I've seen it with my own eyes, they took Lottie, Simon, Sophie.' He gulped. 'They're going to come for me.'

His mum slumped back against the wall, the door swinging open suddenly, almost spilling Bash onto the carpet. She closed her eyes and sighed deeply. It was his voice that did it. He sounded so grown up, so calm and accepting. He sounded like Alex.

She remembered what Alex had said that last time. He had explained to her why he had to go away. It had been just a week before he'd disappeared for good. Bash had been standing outside the door in the torrential rain, waiting like a faithful old dog as Alex explained it to her, all this crazy stuff delivered in a perfectly sane voice. She hadn't wanted to hear it. He was an accountant, not a monster hunter. They had a son and she didn't want to be left alone. But Alex had insisted, explaining it again in his clear voice, leaving no doubt that however much she cried or mocked him, he was going. She had always tolerated his stories and his trips away with Bash. He had a hard job and he needed a break from time to time, but the manic gleam in his eye, the excitement that trembled from every inch of him, well whatever it was he was doing, it wasn't just duty. That was for sure.

She had read the letter that Bash delivered. He had been drunk, tottering on her front step looking half scared to death. It had hurt her so much that the letter was only addressed to Charlie. She knew she was being childish, but she couldn't help it. 'What about me!' she had cried out in anger. Where was her special letter? All she had was a big house, no money and a seven-year-old to feed and clothe. There were no special powers or adventure for her, just the day-to-day responsibility of maintaining normality. Just like it had always been, now she thought about it. Some boys never really grew up and Alex had been no exception.

A few weeks after she had torn up the letter she had fished the pieces from the recycling bin (which on reflection she had subconsciously neglected to put out for collection for three weeks running). She had carefully pieced them back together when Charlie was asleep, bitter tears running down her face as she read over and again the calm and insane last words of her missing husband. And now it was all back again.

Bash stood over to one side of the living room, looking carefully at them. Cathy opened her dark hazel eyes and blew her hair from her face. 'So,' she said firmly, 'What the hell is going on?'

She listened carefully as Charlie explained the events leading up to that day. He started with the creature in the school field and the one he said had sat in his room at night. He talked about the children who had gone missing and the fight that resulted in Sophie being taken. Throughout Bash listened carefully but said nothing, only nodding his encouragement occasionally as Charlie struggled to explain himself.

Her head was spinning. It was one thing to laugh at the stories Alex had told her after he had a few drinks, his manner faintly suggesting he was making it all up. He used to say that he would be killed for telling her all his secrets and she used to laugh along with him. But this was something else entirely. She only had to look at Charlie's suddenly old face to know this was more than a story. Something was happening here. Maybe she had always known, an essential truth hidden in the first throwaway comments Alex had made, not long after they were married. That had all been easier to ignore. Life had carried on and they were happy. The fear in the room today, shattered across Charlie's young/old face, was different. She decided she would listen and then she would be the one to decide what happened next. Not the local drunk.

'And who's this girl?' she asked. 'Mathilda, was it? Do you think we need her here now?'

Bash nodded. 'We do,' he said. 'We need all the help we can get. The Nasties were after Charlie. I'm sure of that and now they have seen that he...'

He paused, trying to find the right words. 'That he wasn't ready to protect himself.'

Charlie winced at his words, looking more miserable by the second. 'I'm sorry, Charlie, I don't mean to upset you but if they think there is a weakness, they're going to go for it. It's a chance to break the bloodline here and now.'

Cathy sighed, pushing her hands through her hair. 'But, Pete, surely you know this is madness. Do you know what you sound like? Whatever it is you think is happening here, even if it's half true, there has to be someone else who can help. The police, the army ...Doctor Who, for Christ's sake? Why does it have to be Charlie?' she pleaded.

Bash opened his mouth to speak, but stopped as he gathered his thoughts. At least she was listening, however dismissive she was. It was now or never. He needed to tell her everything he knew, so she could understand what this was all about and what was at stake. He inwardly cursed Alex for the millionth time for getting him involved in the first place.

'No-one else can help...well actually that might not be true – there may be others, but I don't know who, Alex had a network – a group, they called themselves Watchers if you can believe it – but it all got a bit complicated and I don't know where or who they might be.' He looked carefully into her disbelieving eyes.

'Really, Pete. Watchers. Are you joking? Alex was an accountant who wanted to do something else with his life. He was bored, that was why he made up these things. I told him he should write a book.'

She stared at him, feeling an uncomfortable twinge at the half-truths coming from her mouth, before smothering the feeling with the cold blast of pragmatism that had seen her through all the pressure of the last few years.

'I don't need this, Bash. We don't need this. If Alex thought he was part of some grand group of wizards or something, well that was up to him. If something is killing kids then we need to report it to the police. Tell them what you know.'

'Do you remember when Alex and I used to go away?' he asked suddenly. 'Boys' weekends you used to call them. Well some of them were, you know golf, a few beers, but others were different. He used to drag me off places, but not to get drunk, although God knows I used to do that when I got home. No, he dragged me off hunting these things, these dark evil things.'

His voice thickened and grew hoarse. 'He said they were just little ones – baby ones or something. He enjoyed hunting them, I could see that. Makes a change from counting numbers in the city, I guess, but doing it, seeing it, I think it sent me half crazy, I don't want to go there again but ...but.'

He looked helplessly at Charlie. 'But I can't leave Charlie to fight them alone. I have to help him and that means you have to believe me.'

'I know how this all sounds. I sound crazy. I get it. But the last time, just before he disappeared. He was telling you the truth, trying to level with you. I was drunk—wasn't I always, I told him not to say anything. I said you would divorce him. That was the last time we went hunting together, and the worst.' His voice trailed off.

'How can you expect me to let you bring this to my door, Bash?' replied Cathy. 'I've spent years unpicking the mess Alex left behind. Why shouldn't I just kick you out? I could call the police, you know? I'm sure they would be interested in a weirdo who seems to know so much about the missing kids.'

Bash's eyes flickered from Charlie to Cathy, who returned his broken gaze with eyes chiselled from stone. He didn't know what to say.

'Mum, please. Can we just listen? For me,' Charlie pleaded. 'I know you're angry at Dad, but he told me about this stuff when I was little, I've seen it ever since I was little. I know you can't believe it, but it's real to me. Please, Mum, listen and then decide.'

Cathy felt her anger evaporate. In its place a crushing tiredness threatened to overwhelm her. She closed her eyes.

'Tell us then,' she said. 'Tell us your stupid story and then I can kick you out into the street, hell I'll buy you a bottle of whisky and you can go and drink yourself to death somewhere. Just get it over with and leave.'

Bash looked at Charlie, his eyes watering. 'I don't want to scare you, it's not a nice story.'

'I guess it's a bit late for that,' Cathy said softly, her eyes still closed. 'Tell us.'

Chapter 9

Bash remembered rain lashing against the windscreen of Alex's car, wipers sweeping back and forth at top speed but still struggling to keep up with the torrent. Alex's face was pushed into light and shade by the passing streetlights, grimly determined.

'This is a big one,' Alex had said. 'Maybe the end game.' He looked at him with a strained expression, like someone torn between pleasure and pain.

'I can feel it, Bash, it's under my skin, crawling in my skull and behind my eyes. I don't remember ever feeling it like this before. This is going to be tough, that's why I tried to level with Cathy. Just in case, you know. Matteo said there were so many and so strong.'

'Can't you just leave it then, you know, wait for more reinforcements or something?' he replied. Alex had looked across at him, his eyes suddenly cold and distant. 'No reinforcements, Bash. No waiting. That's not an option.' He reached to his side and passed Bash a small bottle of whisky.

'Drink this,' he had said. 'It's going to be a long night.' Bash had hesitated, if only for a moment, before doing what he was told.

The plane was waiting for them at the small airstrip outside of town. During the summer weekends it was full of people taking to the sky in gliders and microlights, but in the dark winter night it was deserted. The owner of the plane stood under a huge golf umbrella as the rain continued to sweep in from the west, like nails in the glare of the car's headlights as they came to a halt in the small empty car park. The wind buffeted Bash as he opened his door, following Alex who dashed over to the man, coat pulled up over his shoulders and head. By the time they reached him they were soaked to the skin.

'Christ, Alex, where are we going?' he cried as he watched Alex pass a thick wad of banknotes to the old man, who quickly tucked them away inside his heavy overcoat. He turned and walked towards the small airplane that sat at the start of the tarmacked runway. Alex followed behind him, pulling himself through the passenger door that he wrenched open.

'Hurry up, Bash, we need to get moving,' he called, his words torn away by the wind. 'We have a long way to go.'

Bash pulled himself in alongside Alex, his soaking wet clothes sticking to him and leaking into the threadbare seats, water pooling at his feet. The old man pulled some levers and pressed buttons with practised movements, lighting up the dials and buttons across the cockpit of the plane. The engine coughed into life with an alarming number of hitches and stutters, before it smoothed out and the old man taxied down the runway. They trundled along for a moment and then with shocking suddenness the plane lurched up into the night sky.

The flight had been long, and Bash had fallen into a shallow and uncomfortable sleep for much of it, waking only when Alex shook him gently as the plane descended through the dawn sky before landing at another deserted airstrip. The landscape was dusty and unfamiliar. The grey glow of the dawn carried the promise of heat as he followed Alex across the airfield towards the squat figure of a man. Crickets chirped noisily in the long grasses that bordered the dusty runway. Although the sky was lightening, a thin ground mist swirled around Bash's feet as he walked wearily after him. He couldn't pick out the features of the man waiting for them, but as Alex approached him he could see a brief flash of a smile before they embraced, blue light suddenly igniting around them both like a cloak of flickering flame.

The journey continued. An old van now, once white but freckled with rust and faded to a dirty cream, smelling faintly of old cut grass. Bash sat in the cramped cab alongside Alex and the animated figure of Matteo, who spoke rapidly to them in heavily accented English, his hands punctuating each sentence with elaborate gestures. They wound their way up the steep roads taking them into the mountains. As the road grew narrower and Matteo's concentration forced him to silence, Alex spoke quietly to him.

'You remember me telling you a bit about all this stuff, God, it seems so long ago, not long after Charlie was born, and you saw your first one. You remember the brothers and sisters that were born with the flame and how they had separated and formed their own families around the world, watching and waiting for the Nasties.'

Bash nodded; it did ring a very distant bell, but in all honesty he hadn't really paid much attention after his first encounter with a Nastie. Alex had told him all sorts of stuff, but his drinking had been a welcome buffer from the appalling horror. Some of the information had filtered through the haze, but mercifully little.

'When the Nasties come, the families fight them, sometimes on their own and sometimes together. There was a really big surge in the early part of the century, just after the Great War, that had needed all the families to fight together. That must have been a bad one,' he said, frowning.

'Although we're far apart we always resolved to stay connected, so we could be called upon if something went wrong, if it became too much on your part of the Watch. Matteo is part of my family, and together we are responsible for the Watch in Europe. Just the two of us, crazy or what? The Nasties have been quiet for years, flickering in and out of the world but no sign of the Beleth, the Infinite One. No sign of a resurgence. We go hunting, but that was just for fun you know, to keep your eye in.' Alex looked at him, his eyes gleaming briefly. In that moment he had been painfully aware that Alex enjoyed the hunt a bit more than perhaps he should have.

'I haven't spoken with the wider families for years. Not since I tried to find out more about the ways we could hunt them down outside of our own world. They come from somewhere else, I figured we might as well go after them. I know the other Watchers use the thin places, to get through. Even Dad told me a bit about that, but they wouldn't tell me anything. I'm trying to work it out myself, but it's driving me mad, all these secrets when we should be working together. What's the point in sitting around waiting for the monsters to come to us? No-one listened to me, the old fools.' His voice trailed off bitterly.

Alex looked out of the window as Matteo wrested the van around yet another hairpin bend. It had been a surprise when he had contacted him to request his help. They were very similar. Matteo enjoyed the thrill of the hunt and was frustrated with the old ways. He wondered what had happened that he couldn't manage on his own.

The town nestled carefully in the mountains, a winding spiral of narrow paths and pale stone buildings, hanging grimly to the steep cliffs that rose up around it. The morning sun was just starting to crest over the peaks above as Matteo encouraged the protesting van up and around one last sweeping bend into a cobbled courtyard. The van's engine died with a sigh of relief. It was nearly eight o'clock and the town should have been bustling into life. Bash could see the streets leading off from the square, lined with shops all curiously quiet, windows shuttered.

'Where is everyone?' he muttered.

Matteo led them out into the still morning air. The town was eerily silent. There was no birdsong to welcome the new day. In the distance a dog barked, but other than that there was nothing but the soft crunch of gravel underfoot and the slow tick of the van's cooling engine. They followed Matteo to the doorway of an old church.

'The children are all gone,' he explained. 'The ones that haven't been taken, have been shipped off by their parents to safer places. It has happened so very fast.

'We know they emerge every few years – in greater or lesser numbers, small and weak like the ones you enjoy hunting, but this is different, Alex, I have never seen this before. We have kept them subdued for years, but now there is one amongst them that is so big and powerful, and it is spawning so many more. I fear it is the Infinite One, the Beleth returned to us. It has been like a tidal wave of creatures, so hungry; I thought I could contain it but, well, I need your help.'

Matteo knocked on the heavy wooden door of the church, the hooped iron ring striking out a harsh sound in the morning air. After a moment they heard soft shuffling sounds behind the door followed by rasping sound of a bolt being drawn back. The door inched open and a bright blue eye peered at them from behind the door. With a cry of recognition the door was pulled open and they saw the diminutive figure of an elderly priest. 'This,' said Matteo warmly, 'is Father Lucano.' He spoke rapidly to him in Italian as he ushered them into the dim interior of the church.

Soft light filtered through the ornate stained glass window that rose behind the main altar from where the priests would deliver their mass. Dust spiralled down from the vaulted ceiling in the gentle eddying currents of air that whispered through the church, sparkling where it met the shafts of bright morning sunlight.

'I tried to reach the other families as well,' Matteo continued. 'I thought I should let them know what's going on.' The four of them had sat down on the front two pews of the church. Father Lucano listened carefully. Whilst his spoken English was poor, he could follow Matteo's words and nodded occasionally in agreement. 'There was no word, nothing. I tried everything, email, phone, you name it. It's like they've all vanished. Only you replied.'

Father Lucano laid his hand on top of Alex's and softly blessed him, his skin papery thin, but the grip surprisingly firm.

'I don't understand it, Alex,' said Matteo. 'I know we aren't as close as we used to be, but you could always get through to someone. Nothing from Warragul in the Northern Territories, nor Saffya or Chen Lau. It's always been hard to reach Askuwheteau on the reservations but I have tried. We are alone in this, just when we could have done with all of our strength.'

Alex frowned; it had been a while since he had thought to reach out to the family. They had sent him the traditional blessing when Charlie had been born but beyond that he had no contact with anyone other than the occasional call with Matteo, with whom he had always got on well. The elders of the families always seemed to view him with something akin to distrust.

He didn't know why, but it burned in his stomach when he recalled the way he had been ignored when he tried to put forward his views at the council meetings he had attended with his dad. After his dad died he had only been to one more. Since then the hunting he had been doing with Bash was no more than tidying up the odd vagrant Nastie, small stuff really. There had not been a real uprising for many years, even before his father's time, but from what Matteo was saying this was different. The silence from the wider family made him feel a bit uncomfortable.

Bash looked small, hunched in the chair. The retelling of the story had aged him even more, his eyes looked strained and he was trembling slightly. The memories were not good but he wanted to finish it. It was important to him that Cathy knew what Alex had done. He wasn't perfect but in his heart he wanted to do the right thing. He hadn't just left her and Charlie. He had been taken when he was trying to protect them.

'What happened next, Pete?' asked Cathy. Her voice was softened with reluctant interest.

They had left just after midday. The sun was high in the sky and the small town baked in a heat that was stifling and oppressive. Father Lucano had prepared them a simple lunch of bread, meats and cheeses, which none of them had done any more than pick at. Bash had drunk perhaps a little more of the wine than he should have done and although his nerves were soothed, his head felt thick and sluggish as they climbed into Matteo's old van and set off out of town.

'Where are we headed?' he had asked.

'The old orphanage,' replied Matteo. 'It's about four miles from here, we can only drive part of the way, after that we need to walk. I have brought us some drinks – it's a steep climb.'

Bash looked over at the already sleeping figure of Father Lucano, his deeply lined face pressed against the blanket he had fashioned into a pillow and wedged against the window. 'Are you sure the father is up for this?' he asked.

Matteo laughed. 'He is a lot tougher than he looks, my friend, he will not let us down.'

The van struggled up the winding roads, its engine working hard, the cliffs now dropping away with dizzying suddenness on the right-hand side of the road. 'There,' said Matteo suddenly. 'Do you see?'

Up ahead, seemingly born out of the mountain itself, Bash caught sight of the orphanage. It was a jumble of turrets and walls, like a dark fairy tale come to life. Where it sat in the cliff it was steeped in shadow, its placement such that the sun couldn't reach it even in the height of the day.

It looked cold and forbidding, and he felt a shudder twist down his spine. The skin on his arms pulled into gooseflesh despite the stifling heat in the cab of the van. They had put kids in there, he thought, unbelievable. Gradually the road petered out. The broken tarmac was replaced with large stone slabs hewn from the mountain, which caused the van to lurch and bump from side to side, waking a bewildered Father Lucano from his slumber. After a mile or so it was impassable and Matteo pulled the van over to scrubby verge and turned off the engine. The dust blown up by the car tyres pillowed out and hung thickly in the still air. 'Now we walk,' he said.

The path wound its way up through grizzled olive trees and tall pine dipping out of sight here and there. The orphanage looked a long way away. Crickets chirped madly in the long dry grass that spilled onto the dusty path, a constant trilling silenced in inches by their steady progress up the mountainside. 'How do they survive up here?' asked Alex. 'It's in the middle of nowhere.'

'They don't,' replied Matteo. 'The orphanage has been empty for many years. It was closed by the Papal authorities, but not before the scandal had broken.'

Father Lucano nodded grimly at this, as he paced steadily alongside them.

'What scandal?' asked Bash between gasping breaths.

'Priests, children, you understand how it might have been,' Matteo said shortly by way of reply.

Alex and Bash glanced at each other briefly before resuming the steady climb up. It was hard to believe that Alex worked at a desk in the city. A true wolf in sheep's clothing, or at least in a grey suit. In an odd way it was only now that he looked truly happy. The rest of his life was window dressing. This was what he cared about, thought Bash. He knew he himself was just collateral, expendable, but he suddenly felt a faint stab of pity for Cathy. Did she even know who Alex really was? he wondered. A final swig from the bottle of wine left over from lunch helped quell further thoughts. Thinking too deeply seemed an unhelpful distraction at this moment in time.

It was late afternoon by the time they arrived at the iron gates of the orphanage. True to Matteo's word, Father Lucano looked in better shape than they did. Both of them were drenched in sweat, red streaks of dust running in jagged lines down their faces. The gates were warped and rusted, with spindly creepers winding up and through the ornate railings. The courtyard beyond was in shade and the main gate to the building was a forbidding dark mouth. It was completely silent, yet they all felt the presence of something. It hung in the still air like the smell of corrupted flesh. A low buzzing sound, like the throb of a power line cut through the silence, making the fillings in Bash's back teeth throb.

'It's time, Alex,' said Matteo.

Alex flicked his hand out, palm up, a bright blue flame appearing, which he casually manipulated into a ball of boiling brightness by rotating his fingers. Matteo did the same, but in a slightly different way, weaving a disc of light out of strands of blue he appeared to pluck out of the air. Bash could see a small smile playing on Alex's lips and a dancing madness in his eyes.

'Come, Papa,' said Matteo, looking at Father Lucano. 'Get yourself over here and let's see if you still have some use.'

The old priest reached inside his dark cloak and pulled out a metal cross, about six inches long. His long fingers held it out to Matteo, who took it in his hand briefly before he flicked it back to him. It glowed a fantastic blue. The old man smiled as it twirled rapidly in his fingers, flicking it up and into the air where it rotated into a blurring whirr of light. Alex turned to Bash, who pulled his axe from the rucksack over his shoulder. He lit it up, a blue flame roaring soundlessly around its razor sharp edge. Despite himself, and even through the thickness of the wine that coated his senses, Bash felt a hint of the same wild freedom that consumed him the first time he had been out hunting.

'Will I be able to do that?' interrupted Charlie. 'You know, put the flames on things like your axe?'

Bash snapped out of his storytelling and smiled at Charlie. For the first time he looked a little happier, a bit less beaten. That was a good thing.

'You will,' he replied. 'But we will have to practise. I am sure it's not as easy as your dad made it look.' Charlie nodded enthusiastically. Cathy's face pulled into a frown, observing her son's growing enthusiasm for the story Bash was telling.

They had entered the orphanage through a broken window. The main door was locked and had not yielded to their efforts to push it open. 'It was not locked last time,' Matteo muttered to himself.

Whilst Bash, Matteo and Alex had laboured away, Father Lucano had wandered around the building looking for another entrance. The sun was dropping down behind the mountains and the courtyard was growing dimmer as the reflected light from the cliffs around them faded. None of them wanted to be here when it was dark, and the relief on their faces was clear when Father Lucano shouted across to Matteo from the far side of the courtyard that he had found a way in.

Alex boosted himself up and through the window, dropping lightly down into a dark room beyond. There was door on the far side and he quickly checked this was unlocked before he dragged a table across the floor with a protesting squeal to the window. Standing on this he helped the rest of them into the building. They spoke in hushed whispers. 'Where are they?' hissed Alex.

'Last time they were gathering in the crypt underneath the building,' replied Matteo. 'You access it around the back of the altar in the main hall. I should be able to find it from here, although I didn't come this way last time and when I left it was in a hurry,' he said with a grimace.

'Hurry' did not even begin to describe the frantic speed by which he'd departed last time, throwing disc after disc of burning blue over and around him as hordes of Nasties had descended from the rafters like bats at dusk. He didn't think further description would be helpful at this stage. They were nervous enough as it was.

They followed Matteo carefully down a long hallway, the plaster on the walls fractured, fallen away in places to reveal the bare stone walls beneath. Dusty oil lamps lined the corridor that led to another door at the far end.

They crept along, illuminated by the blue flames emanating ever more brightly around Alex and Matteo. Father Lucano whispered a prayer under his breath in Latin, his eyes fixed forward. Bash's heart pounded in his chest, his hands gripping the axe so tightly his knuckles glowed white in the neon light. From ahead they could hear a clamouring scrabble of claws, and a slowly building shriek – like the call of swifts in summer, but growing in intensity, ever louder until by the time Alex placed his hand on the door and looked back at them pale and sweating, they could barely hear him as he asked, 'Ready?'

It had all happened very quickly.

He pushed the door open and the four men darted quickly through the gap and into the altar room of the orphanage's chapel. The scene that met them was of utter, bewildering chaos. A flurry of moving shapes and sweeping blackness, spewing forth from a huge crater that had opened up in the floor above the defiled crypt. The pews, where children had once sat in contemplation, had been thrown up into the air with such force that they had been shattered against the walls, splinters of timber littering the floor and impaled into ceiling. And everywhere the Nasties crawled, more than Alex had ever seen, clambering over each other like locusts. For a moment they were struck dumb by the scale of what they were seeing.

Bash staggered back in horror, his mouth open. This was nothing like what he had seen before. He felt his mind tearing away at the edges as his eyes tried to make sense of the insanity before him. The Nasties turned to them as one, a collective sweep of bodies, red eyes breaking open in the blackness, followed by a shattering roar of hatred.

Father Lucano broke the paralysis, leaping forward, his cross held in front of him glowing a dazzling blue. With a grace that belied his age he leaped up and onto the nearest fallen pew, before hurling the cross in a whirl of light straight at the horde of advancing Nasties. The cross cut through the nearest like a blade, splitting one clean in half and then whirring away and back to his outstretched hand, like a magical boomerang. The Nasties howled in anger and surged forward.

It became difficult to see what was happening, so thick were their numbers, leaping and twisting down on them. Blue flames bounced against the walls, smashing into them. Bash swung his axe in huge sweeping arcs, the blade slicing into any Nasties that got in his way. Later he wouldn't be able to lift his arms above his waist but for now he felt nothing – just an overpowering terror that had wiped his mind clear of thought. All he wanted to do was reach Alex, who was now crouching in front of a stricken Matteo, who had fallen with a vicious cut running down his side.

Alex was doing his best to protect him but still more Nasties scrambled out of the crater in the floor. He arrived, his axe vibrating from a blow struck against a larger Nastie that fell screeching to the floor. As he did so a hush began to descend in the room, the Nasties pulling back slightly and silencing their shrieks of rage. He could now hear Matteo's curses, the gasping breath of Father Lucano and the soft scratching of claws as the Nasties moved restlessly in front of them.

The reason for the hiatus became apparent. A huge hand formed out of the crater and clawed into the stone floor, followed by another as thick, muscled arms pulled an enormous creature up into the church. The nearest Bash's mind could make sense of its shape was to liken it to a massive gorilla, but its arms were long and seemingly capable of stretching to insane proportions. Its head shifted and moved, eyes splitting open insect-like, before focusing on the four men. It blinked, the eyelids flicking over its red eyes, before its mouth tore open revealing an endless row of needle-sharp teeth. It screamed its anger.

Alex looked on in absolute horror. The thing coming out of the pit was worse than all the stories, it could only be the Infinite One, Beleth, here and now, a legend made flesh.

The number of Nasties that flocked around it were in themselves unprecedented, but they were like the ones he had seen and killed before. But Beleth was something else. Matteo had just talked about how there were too many for him to manage alone, but he now realised this was much more than that. For perhaps the first time he felt really afraid. They were out of their depth.

He shouted to be heard above the screams echoing around the room. 'Bash, help me get Matteo up, we need to get out of here.'

Matteo called over to Father Lucano as he staggered to his feet, holding his side, but the noise had risen to such a deafening level that he didn't hear.

The Nasties descended again and all was chaos.

Bash remembered little of what happened next. He saw the huge creature swipe its arm across the room, sweeping some of the smaller Nasties away before catching Father Lucano full in the face. He flew through the air and hit the wall at the back of the room, slumping to the floor with blood running thickly from a deep wound in his head. His cross fell to the floor with a metallic clatter that they heard above the noise in the room.

Matteo screamed in anguish and pulled free of them as they desperately tried to hold the horde of Nasties at bay. Bright bolts of blue flame smashed into creatures, who exploded into nothingness. He reached the fallen figure of Father Lucano, cradling him gently as Alex threw ball after ball of flame at the Nasties that crowded towards the two stricken men. Matteo's face contorted with rage, as he gently laid the old man on the floor. With the last of his strength he pulled himself up on one of the broken pews and began firing his discs of blue light in all directions, screaming his fury as the tears ran down his face.

The Beleth roared in defiance, twisting out of shape and spiralling like a black, oily smoke through the air towards him. As it descended, its physical presence thickened once more and Matteo desperately fired more flame towards it. Alex did the same, the combined force of their power now searing chunks of blackened flesh from its body.

But its progress and intentions were unstoppable. With a roar of triumph its head and jaws stretched out and closed with a crunch over Matteo's head, snapping tightly shut at his waist, shaking him briefly from side to side like a dog, before releasing his broken body.

Alex mouth opened, but terror had robbed him of speech. On instinct he unleashed an enormous torrent of flame which poured from his hands in the direction of the Beleth. Bash was weeping with fear, but hacked and cut into the smaller creatures that leapt down towards them. Alex's assault was starting to make an impact. Beleth howled with pain, its black flesh sheering off as the blue flames tore over and around it like a whirlwind. Alex shouted in desperation to Bash, his eyes wide with fear. 'We have to get out, Bash, I can't hold it for much longer.'

Bash ran over to where Matteo lay, face down on the floor. He rolled him gently over. Like Father Lucano, he was dead. The number of Nasties had diminished. Between them they had killed hundreds. All that remained were smears of thick black liquid, pooling in the uneven floor like rivers of bitter treacle.

Beleth staggered back under Alex's continued attack, shaking its massive head back and forth, its mouth torn into a rictus of pain and anger. In an instant its form loosened, spiralling suddenly into a black whirlwind that disappeared up into the shadows of the ceiling, the remaining smaller Nasties joining it until their screams diminished into nothing.

Alex collapsed to the floor, exhausted. It was over.

The journey home was a hazy memory of exhaustion and pain. They had loaded the broken bodies of Father Lucano and Matteo into the van, laying them carefully onto the back seat. Carrying them down the mountain had been backbreaking, but Alex had insisted they couldn't be left in that poisoned place.

'At least we won, Alex, that thing, it's gone, you killed it,' said Bash as he started the van and turned it carefully round in the narrow track. Alex had said nothing, his face a mask of exhaustion, but he looked scared.

Bash looked up at Cathy and Charlie. 'Alex knew that Beleth wasn't dead. It would be back for him, and for Charlie. I don't think he had the strength to kill it on his own and I don't know what happened, but I think he had to sacrifice himself somehow to send it away and protect you. He said he was alone now. With Matteo dead there was no-one but him to hold back the tide. That's why he gave the letter and that old necklace to me. A week later he was gone.'

Cathy stared intently at Bash. 'You really think this is real, don't you? And you say they're back, these Nasties and they want Charlie?'

'They're coming, I know it.' Bash looked at them, his face a mask of determination. 'Whether you believe me or not I need to make sure Charlie is ready.'

Chapter 10

It was Saturday morning and Aunt Val was getting ready to go to the shops. She liked to dress up a bit on the weekends and take the bus to Guildford with her friends, and the earlier she could get away the better. The first bus could be picked up at eight-thirty from the end of the street and so when she bustled out of the house Mathilda was still in bed.

Mathilda hadn't been sleeping well since the attack. Her dreams were vivid and horrible. In them Charlie was taken and killed along with the other children, whilst she was frozen to the spot, unable to help. In others it was like she was inside the body of Esther (which was horrible anyway), shockingly handing over Sophie to a dribbling beast which tore her to pieces in front of her eyes.

It was only in the morning, as light began to appear along the edges of her curtains and the birds began to sing their first songs, that she was able to fall into a light, troubled sleep. So when the doorbell rang stridently, the sharp tone bouncing up the stairs, her first reaction was to bury her head still further under her duvet and hope it would go away.

The bell rang again, followed by the creak of the letterbox opening and Charlie's voice calling, 'Mathilda – are you there?' She had no option but to pull herself out of bed and stagger sleepily down the stairs to the door.

When she opened it she was surprised to see not only Charlie, but Bash and a lady who could only be his mum, all standing together in the porch. She pushed her hair out of her eyes and tightened her dressing gown around her, smiling uncertainly. 'Can we come in then?' asked Bash.

Cathy watched Mathilda curl her long legs underneath her on the sofa. She thought she was very pretty and looked a lot older than fourteen, but they all did these days. Considering what they were discussing, she also seemed very composed. She had hardly raised an eyebrow when Bash had suggested that she go to the school and retrieve her bow. She only intervened to explain how she could get in despite it being a weekend.

'It's a stroke of luck,' said Mathilda. 'The school is having some work done and I know the builders are in there over the weekends. I should be able to sneak in and I know where Mr Jones keeps the keys to the gym equipment. He trusts me to close it up after practice.'

Her face took on a slightly guilty cast, but in truth she was excited by the prospect of getting her bow and also having the chance to shoot it at something more interesting than straw targets. The thought of being a hunter, a hero – like that girl in *The Hunger Games* – was not without some appeal.

'You should stay here,' she said. 'My aunt will be out all day and it will be less conspicuous if it is just me creeping around.' She pulled a long sports bag out from under the stairs and quickly removed the hockey sticks and pads that filled it, swinging it over her shoulder. 'I won't be long.'

For Bash the priority was to get Charlie back in the game. He needed time to practise and get his confidence back after the shock of the last attack. It was a matter of life and death in truth, although he was careful not to say this in front of Cathy, especially now she was in fragile agreement to the course of action he had proposed. He was sure that the Nasties and in particular the big one, the one called Beleth, was going to make its move before long. Charlie had to be ready.

For her part Cathy just listened with a mixture of dizzying anxiety and a resigned acceptance of the insanity of it all. All she wanted was Charlie to be safe. If that meant following Bash and the girl, Mathilda, around until this was done (whatever that meant) then she had decided that was what she would do.

It was an anxious wait. Not least because Cathy was wondering what on earth Mathilda's aunt would make of it if she came home early to find them sitting awkwardly in her front room. Bash had cleaned himself up a bit, but no amount of window dressing could hide the slightly manic look in his eyes. He still looked like the type of person you would cross the street to avoid.

Charlie said little. He was thinking about whether he would be able to call the flame up when the time came. Compared to how he had felt the first time when he put amulet on, it now seemed as though that power was buried deep inside. He knew his nerves were not helping and he needed to relax but it was impossible. Whatever Bash said he could see the doubt and concern in all their eyes, which only served to make him even more worried. Without him they were at the mercy of the Nasties, and that burden was a heavy one.

Mathilda came back just before eleven o'clock, the colour high in her cheeks. It had been very exciting sneaking through the deserted school. Everything had seemed different – like she was in a film or something. The builders didn't see her, she had moved with silent grace along the corridors, retrieving her bow and a quiver which she filled with the best arrows they had, the ones Mr Jones had ordered especially for her. She would need to sneak it back at some point, but that worry was for another day.

'What now?' she asked, pulling the bow from her hockey bag. She caught sight of herself in the mirror above the fireplace and couldn't help but smile. She looked like a warrior.

'We go to my place,' said Bash. 'It's out of the way and there's some space out the back to practise.'

Charlie smiled weakly. He looked pale and worried as he followed them out of the door to his mum's car, which she had parked just down the road. She put a comforting arm around his shoulder as they walked and gave him a squeeze, although she was equally bewildered by the pace of events. What were they getting into? she thought as she started the little car and pulled away.

Bash's house was a little tidier than the last time they visited. In any event the empty bottles had been cleared away and the windows were open, with the breeze freshening the stale rooms. He had swept over the floor the day before, but he still looked a little embarrassed at the state of the place as he ushered them through the house and out of the old French doors that led into the overgrown garden. Cathy goggled slightly at the mass of weeds that had invaded the lawn and pushed their way up and through the paving slabs of the patio where she and Alex had shared a glass of wine with him many summers ago.

The air of neglect around the house, peeling paint and faded curtains, was a sign of how far Bash had fallen in the last few years. She felt a stab of guilt as she wondered what he had been through. Alex's sudden departure had left a lot of damage, more than she had even suspected.

The garden was long and secluded. The lawn was waist high in places, with clumps of dying grass supporting vast alien ant nests, before it opened out at the end where it headed towards the trees that flanked the back fence. The thick hedges that ran down both sides ensured they were not overlooked. Bash led the way, breaking the path through the grass, with the rest of them following behind. The late afternoon air was thick with insects that buzzed and fizzed through the air around them. The initial coolness of the spring had turned into an unseasonably warm early summer, and sweat ran steadily down Bash's face. Mathilda's bow kept catching on the high stems, and she took to holding it above her head. *What a sight we must look*, Cathy thought as they reached the clearing under the trees, where the grass and weeds had been unable to take hold in the shadows.

'What now?' asked Charlie. He wanted to get started, but at the same time was worried about whether he would be able to do what Bash wanted. What if he was rubbish, what if he couldn't do it, he thought? He tried to look relaxed but could feel his mum staring at him. She would know what he was thinking, she always did.

Bash frowned. This was tricky. He knew a bit about what Alex had been able to do, but at the end of the day he was always just the helper, the supporting act. It had been Alex that led the way. But he had promised Charlie and Cathy that he could help, that he had answers. They were relying on him.

'Do you remember what your dad wrote in the letter, Charlie?' asked Bash.

Charlie nodded, drawing a surprised look from his mum. 'You've seen the letter, Charlie? How?'

Charlie's face flushed red. 'I'm so sorry, Mum, I took it from under your bed, and the amulet, I read it all and it started to work, but I didn't mean to, I'm sorry.' His voice thickened into tears. She pulled him to her and held him tight.

'It's alright, Charlie,' she said softly. 'The letter was meant for you anyway, I just didn't know when would be the right time for you to read it. It was all a bit crazy. I should have shown it to you sooner.'

Bash and Mathilda looked on awkwardly. 'It was my idea he put on the amulet, I was with him,' said Mathilda.

'You put it on Charlie?' said Cathy. 'What happened?'

He struggled to explain the feeling that had come over him when he had put the amulet on. If he had been older he might have had the words, he remembered the rush of power that accompanied a cycling up of energy in his body. It had been like starting an engine, but an immensely powerful one. It had felt beyond him, beyond anything really. Like being Superman or something, but better. If he could have, he would have explained it felt limitless. Like he could do anything. Like blue flames were maybe the tip of the iceberg.

'It burned into me and I felt something strange, you know, like a connection,' he replied. 'Like a car starting or something. Whatever – but it fired up a part of me and a flame came up into my hands. It was pretty cool,' he finished rather lamely.

'Go on, Charlie,' encouraged Cathy. She had read the letter a million times, dismissing its contents, wilfully ignoring them in truth. She certainly hadn't mentioned it to the police when they had questioned her. What good would that have done? She had far too much on her plate to give much credence to the crazy story in Alex's letter.

'In the letter Dad just said to concentrate, relax and allow it to come and it did, it was easy then, but the other day when those things took Sophie it wouldn't come – it...' He paused, his voice losing its urgency. 'I was too scared.' He looked down at the floor, pushing the dead leaves around with his feet.

Bash hunched down in front of him and put his hands gently on his shoulders. 'Charlie, you've got to stop blaming yourself, we start again today. We're all here to help you.'

He took a deep breath and looked up at his mum, who forced a smile and nodded supportively. 'OK, I'll give it a go, what have I got to lose?' he said.

Quite a lot, thought Bash.

Charlie was starting to feel a little stupid. He had been standing in the middle of a loose circle formed by Bash, his mum and Mathilda for about twenty minutes now. He was holding his hands out in front of him, palms up like he had the day he had put the amulet on. He was breathing deeply (as his mum suggested). Thinking of the flame (as Mathilda suggested), and trying to stay relaxed (as Bash mentioned continuously, which was not very relaxing in truth), but nothing was happening. He could feel something, a tightness in the centre of his chest and a fluttering in his stomach, but the burst of raw power that had flowed around him that first time was absent. In truth he just wanted to be left alone now. He was tired of them looking at him and he was starting to hear a very slight tinge of exasperation in Bash's repeated calls to 'relax'. He wondered if this power of his had gone, maybe moved on to someone capable of dealing with it. After another ten minutes, he decided enough was enough.

'Can you leave me alone for a bit please?' he said as he dropped his hands to his sides and opened his eyes. 'This isn't working, I don't feel anything. I just want to be left alone.'

'You have to keep trying, Charlie. Those things are out there now and they will be coming back. I don't want to scare you or your mum,' said Bash, glancing at Cathy. 'But that's the reality of it, we need you to find a way to unlock it again.'

Charlie felt the first twinge of annoyance. If it was so easy why couldn't they do it? His stomach twisted slightly as he turned to look at Bash, and harsh words bubbled up to his lips. 'I'm done with this, I just want to go home,' he said. 'None of you have any idea how this feels, you're just stood there looking at me and I just feel stupid.'

Charlie ran back to the house through the long grass. His mum followed behind him. Bash looked at Mathilda, bewildered. The trees behind them rustled secretively, as a breeze picked up and blew away the stagnant afternoon air. He didn't know what to do. He shuddered at the thought of what waited for them all out there.

'Come on, Mathilda,' he said. 'Let's go back inside and see if he's alright.'

She looked at him awkwardly, not really knowing what to say. It was all very well insisting that Charlie practise and she understood the urgency, but she couldn't blame him for wanting out. She hated being the centre of attention as well. If Bash had any sense he would leave him alone for a bit, she thought.

Chapter 11

The evening drew in. Charlie and his mum sat together on the old sofa in front of the fire, the flickering flames providing light and warmth. The electricity was still off and they listened to the wood crackle and pop in the gloom. The others had gone into town to collect something to eat, Bash carefully backing Cathy's car out of the drive with a promise to drive sensibly. Charlie had wanted to go home but Bash had convinced him they were safer together. At least if he was here they could try again tomorrow, thought Bash. He couldn't shake an increasing sense of urgency. The Nasties were coming, he could feel it.

Cathy ran her hand through Charlie's hair as he sat next to her looking at the fire. He was only ten, she thought, everyone assumed he was older because of his size, and whilst he was pretty grown up for his age (he'd had to grow up fast when Alex disappeared), he was still her little boy and she couldn't bear to see him looking so frightened. Even more so she didn't like the growing pressure on him to deliver on his so-called powers.

She had agreed to stay with Mathilda and Bash, because she was shaken by all the information and Charlie's insistence that it was real, but she would have preferred to get him home and away from all of this. Mathilda had called her aunt, telling her she was staying at a friend's house, and Cathy felt compelled to stay put. Charlie had said very little since he had run into the house and she was relieved when Bash and Mathilda had decided to go into town for food. She hoped it would give her the chance to talk to him alone. She could tell he needed to relax, to find some sense of himself again. But he had said little, providing single-word answers to her questions. If anything he looked even worse, his eyes constantly straying to the darkening sky outside the window.

Charlie was feeling nervous, but he couldn't say anything to his mum. She was looking at him constantly, they all were, and it was doing his head in. His body was so tense. He couldn't relax, however much Bash kept saying to. He could feel the muscles in his arms and legs jumping and twitching. His eyes moved restlessly around the room, inevitably coming back to the view out of the window to the front of the house. It was getting dark, and the first streetlamp some way down the road was flickering into life. Bash's house was a long way from the main village and the lights were few and far between. He thought it would be pitch black out here when it got properly dark. A log on the fire popped suddenly, spitting sparks out onto the heavy rug in front of it. A smell like burning hair filled the room, acrid and unpleasant. 'I'm going to get a drink of water,' said his mum, lifting her arm from around his shoulder and pushing herself up from the creaking sofa. 'Do you want one?' she asked.

He shook his head slightly, allowing himself to sink back into the chair. His mum left the room and headed for the kitchen at the rear of the house. He got up and walked over to the window. He gripped the windowsill tightly as he peered out, looking down the drive, the feeling of nervousness intensifying. There was something odd about the shadows that thickened around the hedge that bordered the front of the house. They were darker than the evening gloom would necessitate. It felt like the night was closing in on Bash's house quicker than everywhere else, like the dark had business with them that couldn't wait. He hoped Bash wouldn't be long. There was no denying it, he felt like they were being watched.

In the woods that surrounded the house the Nasties gathered. Beleth squatted at the edges of the shadowed ground beneath the trees. Around it smaller Nasties moved and capered. The horde varied in size, the largest the size of a big dog, the smallest like a rat or ferret. Beleth towered above them, having born them all from its flesh, spawning more and more as it sought to increase their number. The process of spawning was painful and draining, particularly now what remained of the girl had been eaten. It took great energy to keep respawning and more food was required if the process was to continue, but for now it was satisfied that it was worthwhile. It needed more support. The desire to spawn was instinctive. It was sure the boy was weak but it would not risk itself yet, far better to sacrifice some of the horde first – to test the boy again, maybe even finish it here and now.

It had lived forever, far beyond the brief sacrificial life of its young. The horde it had gathered in Italy those years ago had been tremendous, gorged on the sustenance provided by numerous children, but even that had not been enough to kill those who came for them. Beleth had fled that day, leaving its kin dying around it, but it had seen the Watcher was vulnerable, it had tasted his fear for his son, and that had made him weak and foolish. Foolish enough to try to finish Beleth without his full strength, without his talisman and so he had been crushed, his withered body relinquishing its flame for the last time in the echoing emptiness of the inter world. But at great cost. Beleth had fallen back into its world of shadows with a myriad wounds. It had been close, far closer than it had expected and it had cursed its own weakness in allowing itself to be vulnerable after all the care it had taken to finish the Watchers off for good. But now the signs were good. The boy was weak and had done nothing to protect his friends last time. The old man's magic had faded from his axe and there was no-one out there to help them. It had seen to that. The family was broken, it had finished the Watchers off in the world. Only one remained all the way over the other side of the world and he had also been compromised. Even the Watchers could fall prey to the pressure of living in the new world. They could be turned and used just like the rest of the sheep that formed the human race.

The Beleth was not the senseless creature that the Watchers believed. It could think and plan when required, it understood the changing shape of the world on which it existed and in many ways was better equipped to adapt to the relentless change that had wrought this planet. The Watchers were of an older time, when a magic man would be a person of importance, respected, but the modern world had nothing for them, they were isolated and unrecognised. Forced to hide their real gifts, they made themselves susceptible to temptation and so they had fallen one by one. The Nasties' time was drawing near again, and with the death of this boy there would be a return to the old chaos, a time when its kind could feed again and again. The thought made it grin, a vast crescent of teeth shining in the near dark. Maybe the new age would start tonight, Beleth speculated. That was a pleasant thought.

Chapter 12

Cathy stood at the sink overlooking the garden, washing a grimy cup that she had taken from one of the kitchen cupboards. She stared at her reflection in the glass, her thoughts turning restlessly over in her head when the window suddenly shattered inwards. Something heavy hit her square in the chest and she fell backwards, landing on the broken glass with a scream. She felt something else land on the floor next to her, the glass skittering away across the tiled floor as claws scrambled for purchase.

Charlie heard the window break and his mum scream. He spun round from the window and in the flickering firelight he saw the first of the Nasties skid into the doorway, a further five or six quickly joining it, jostling for position as they moved carefully forward, snarling and spitting from malformed faces. He felt a spike of terror as the creatures moving smoothly towards him. The nearest leapt nimbly up onto the back of the sofa, its claws puncturing the worn fabric. The others moved fluidly around it, shadows of oily black. He stumbled back against the window frame. There was nowhere to go.

Cathy picked herself up from the kitchen floor, barely registering the smear of thick blood that covered the hand that she swiped across her forehead. 'Charlie,' she called, moving out of the kitchen and down the hall. The flickering light of the fire cast dancing shadows against the wall. As she approached the doorway she could see him pushed up against the window, his face contorted with terror. She couldn't see anything unusual in the room, although it looked wrong to her eyes, distorted. It was like she was seeing something out of the corner of her eye – black shapes – but each time she tried to focus on them, they danced away. It was making her feel dizzy and nauseous.

'Charlie – are you OK?' she managed between deep breaths.

'Mum, stay back, please – they're here,' he gasped.

The Nasties turned to look at the woman. She stood holding the doorframe as if for support, like she was on the deck of a ship rolling in rough seas. Food, but not what they wanted, an annoyance to be disposed of, but nothing more.

The larger of them flicked its head in her direction, and two of the smaller Nasties moved off towards her, teeth bared.

Cathy was doing her best to stand up. The room in front of her rolled and swayed in her vision. It was as if she was drunk, her eyes spinning up and away each time she tried to focus. With all her strength she focused on Charlie, the flickering darkness of the room narrowing to a point around his terrified face.

He watched as the two Nasties approached his mum. Her face was pale and she looked sick. The larger Nasties moved carefully towards him. He had to do something, he thought, his mind filled with sudden visions of his mum being torn apart. He wouldn't lose both his parents, he couldn't. He cried out, his anger quelling the panic, and with it a feeling of enormous energy welled up from his stomach. The Nasties were almost upon him when the flames that had been so stubbornly hidden earlier suddenly poured from him, a rush of coolness pulsing up his spine, followed by an irresistible burst of energy flowing over his shoulders and down his arms to his fingertips. He looked down at his hands, moving his fingers carefully as strands of liquid blue flame stretched between them like gossamer spider webs. The power was so much stronger than last time, the blue glow spreading rapidly around his whole body.

With a snarl Charlie pushed the energy he felt itching in his fingertips out at the nearest Nastie, noting with satisfaction the look of bewildered fear that flickered across its distorted features as the blue flame burned over and around it, reducing it to a charred and bubbling smear of foul flesh. The flame rolled around his hands and he fired again at the two Nasties that were leaping at his mum, enveloping them, their black shapes frozen in a flash of brilliant blue before exploding with a splatter of gore that covered his mum from head to foot. The remaining Nasties leapt at him, a razor-sharp talon cutting through his shirt and searing the skin underneath, causing him to cry out in pain. A further Nastie clawed at his face, tearing the skin on his forehead, the blood flowing thickly into his eyes. The initial euphoria that accompanied the destruction of the Nasties was swamped by a feeling of panic as yet another leapt upon him. Their teeth and claws pulled and tore at him and with the blood stinging furiously in his eyes, he couldn't see what he was doing. He flailed around with his hands, the blue flames washing over them ineffectually, without direction.

Cathy could see Charlie struggling on the floor. Shapes shifted and flickered about him as she picked herself up. Something was here, but her mind continued to deny the truth. She swiped at her face, blood and sweat mixing and causing her eyes to sting.

The Nasties moved around him like snakes, striking at him with elongated talons that stretched out on improbably long arms. One held fast over his shoulders and was trying to claw through the brilliant blue light that still surrounded him. The flames burned it, but it was a willing sacrifice. He was weakening. The protective blue flames were being torn from around him, floating away and dissolving like wisps of smoke.

Cathy ran to him, without thought, reaching to grab hold of him, but instead sinking her hands into a flesh that was boiling hot and yielding. A look of horror raced across her face, but still the truth flickered and danced away from her eyes. A line of blood raced up her arm. A further laceration crisscrossed her thigh, searing pain following behind. She pulled with all her strength, oblivious to the talons now sinking into her leg as one of the other Nasties grabbed at her. Unseen, the creature's flesh pulled away into her hands, stretching like hot toffee into a strand of black that grew longer still as she was dragged rapidly away from him by the Nastie holding her leg. Although small, the Nastie was enormously strong and it tossed her across the room with ease. Her hands remained tightly closed on the flesh of Charlie's attacker and the momentum of her descent jerked it suddenly off his back. She landed in a heap next to the fireplace.

Charlie pulled himself to his feet and saw his mum wrestling with a black creature, rapidly forming itself into a coherent shape of talons and fangs. From somewhere he found new reserves of strength and without thinking blasted a bolt of flame out from his hands that seared through the one nearest to him, cutting a hole about the size of a football through its middle before enveloping the creature holding his mum. The one remaining Nastie backed away snarling and spitting. Its blood red eyes flickered left to right, exploring a way out. He walked steadily towards it, the blue flame enveloping him flickering, his hands unconsciously fashioning a ball of flame that burned bright, its light reflecting back in the uncertain eyes of the creature. Before he had time to attack the creature spun and elongated up towards the ceiling, disappearing in a whirlwind of black. The blue flame in his hand flickered out, the shroud of light around him fading as he collapsed to the floor.

When Bash and Mathilda returned, carrying a thin white carrier bag containing cartons of Chinese food, they found Cathy cradling the still form of Charlie by the fire. She was barely recognizable, her clothes torn, her skin cut and bruised. The air in the room was thick with a meaty smell, underpinned by panic and sweat. Charlie was either asleep or in a dead faint. The food dropped to the floor as Bash rushed over to them, recognising the bubbling carcass of a Nastie ingrained into the floor next to the sofa.

'God, Cathy – what happened?' She looked at him blankly. 'They, they were here,' she muttered before fainting herself.

Bash picked through the cold fried rice without much enthusiasm. They were both asleep in his bed. He had carried them upstairs, carefully washing the worst of the foul sludge from Cathy's face before putting them in his room, where he hoped they would get some sleep and recover. Charlie had stirred briefly, smiling at him as he laid him down, which had given him a little hope that he would be OK. At least he had managed to access his powers, otherwise who knew what they would have returned to.

Mathilda had busied herself making bandages from old sheets she found in a cupboard to dress the puncture wounds on Cathy's leg and to clean the deep gash on Charlie's forehead. Throughout neither had woken and by the time she had finished it was late into the night. Mathilda camped out on the floor next to the double bed where Cathy and Charlie slept. Bash sat in a chair by the window, watching carefully with his axe held tightly in his lap. He didn't think they would be back tonight. Charlie had given them something to think about, he thought grimly. His axe was mute in his hands, without even a flicker of the blue flame, but its presence reassured him. He sighed deeply; it looked like it was going to be a long night.

Chapter 13

Charlie was woken by the gentle cooing of a pigeon on the roof of the house, the sound echoing down the chimney into the bedroom. In the chair by the window Bash was asleep snoring softly, his head slumped onto his chest. He could hear the steady breathing of his mum next to him and from the corner of his eye saw what could only be Mathilda's feet poking out from under a blanket on the floor. His left eye opened reluctantly, the lid gummed shut by dried blood that had flowed from his forehead during the night. The makeshift bandage that Mathilda had applied was next to him on the bed, dislodged by his movement. Despite the wound in his head, he felt surprisingly good. His body didn't ache and the cut on his head was not sore. Carefully, so as not to wake the others, and after briefly checking his mum more closely, he climbed out of bed and crept across the room and out of the door, before heading downstairs.

The clock in the hall showed it was just after seven. He peeked into the living room, the images of the night before now rushing back into his head. He could see the pools of black blood and gore on the floor by the fireplace and around the window where he had fought, as well as splattered up the wall and doorframe. It smelled bad, but on closer inspection he could see the evidence of the Nasties was fading with the first touches of sunlight that broke through the gaps in the curtains and hit the floor. The black ooze was lifting up in fragments and evaporating into the air. He pulled back the curtains fully and within minutes the room was clear.

He looked at his hands and could see a ripple of blue flame between his fingers, gently rolling around him, as if he had dipped them in paraffin and set them alight. The flame was all around him, a soft covering of blue flickering about an inch around his whole body. With a flick of his hand a ball of flame erupted and sat hovering over his upturned palm, tracking his hand as he moved it back and forth in front of him. His eyes glowed a bright blue and as he grinned the light around him grew brighter still until he was a dazzling blaze of blue. This was better than *Call of Duty*. He felt unstoppable.

Bash awoke with a slow blink, his eyes focusing reluctantly, his neck and back screaming at him as he tried to sit up straight. Rubbing his eyes furiously, he noticed Charlie was gone.

'Charlie,' he called. The sound of his voice woke Cathy and caused Mathilda to stir under her blanket. He continued calling as he ran down the stairs, Cathy following anxiously behind him. Charlie was not in the living room. With increasing anxiety they checked the rest of the rooms, as he ran his hands through his hair, muttering.

Cathy saw him first and stopped dead in her tracks, her mouth dropping open slightly. Bash ran back into the kitchen and followed her gaze out to the garden, where Charlie stood, a beacon of burning blue flame in the shape of a boy. Above him balls of flame circled, spiralling around him like atoms orbiting a nucleus.

Cathy looked at Bass in astonishment. 'What the... is this what Alex could do?'

'I never saw anything like this,' Bash replied. 'This, this is incredible'

The power emanating from him was palpable when they opened the back door and walked out towards him. The air felt almost thick with some kind of electrical charge. It made their hair crackle with static and teeth ache. He had his back to them and was lazily rotating the balls of blue flame above his head, oblivious to their approach.

It had been so easy to connect with the energy, thought Charlie as he conjured up another ball of flame to add to the others, He held them in a spiralling flight pattern above his head. He wondered why it hadn't been there before, when it mattered. His mood darkened momentarily as he thought of Sophie and her screams as she was taken. That wouldn't happen again, he thought. There would be no more mistakes. He heard a noise behind him and spun round, the balls of flame rotating with him and streaking out towards Bash and his mum, who flinched, alarmed. In an instant they stopped, hanging again in mid-air, like obedient dogs waiting for his command. He looked at them and smiled, his eyes flashing a brilliant blue.

'Hi, Mum, Bash,' he said, noticing identical expressions of shock. He allowed the balls of flame to drop down into his hands, falling rapidly onto his palm, absorbing one into the next, until a single one remained, its light so bright you could barely look at it.

'You've been busy,' said Bash with a slight smile, before Cathy interrupted with a flood of questions as she ran towards him and held him tight. It was only after she grabbed him that she thought of the flames that surrounded him. She looked at him in wonder, she couldn't feel them at all. 'Oh, Charlie, what have you been doing, I don't know what to say about last night, I can't believe all this and your face is so cut, what can...'

Charlie looked over at Bash, feeling slightly awkward as his mum continued to hug him tight and pour more questions at him. He was pretty sure she would run out of steam soon, her questions were diminishing, and after a moment or two she stepped back from him, looking at him carefully. 'Are you OK?' she said meaningfully.

'I'm fine, Mum – I feel good.' He paused. 'I feel strong, you know.'

'We need to get you out of here, back home where you'll be safe, where we will both be safe. I'm sorry, Bash,' Cathy continued, turning to him. 'This is not going to happen, we are going home. I will call the police, get some real people involved – this is not something that can be dealt with by a ten-year-old.'

Her voice was rising steadily as she struggled to keep control of her emotions. The horror of the previous night was starting to overcome her. Taking Charlie firmly by the hand, she started to head back to the house.

Charlie stood firm. She pulled on his arm like someone trying to drag a naughty dog down the street. He carefully unpicked her fingers.

'No, Mum,' he said. 'We need to stay put. It's like Bash said, they're going to come back. They will always come back. And while we are waiting they will need to feed, which just means more kids are going to be killed. I don't want this any more than you do, but I have to face them and stop the killing, it's just me and whoever can help, and I'm going to do it whatever – you can't stop me.'

'What about the other ones then?' she said, her voice watery with despair. 'The other Watchers. Can't they help?' She looked at Bash. 'It can't just be us, just Charlie. This is madness. We nearly died last night, don't you understand?'

'I don't know how to contact anyone, Cathy,' said Bash quietly. 'Alex never told me how, and from what happened last time it sounded like they were gone anyway. There isn't anyone to help. You could go to the police, but say what? They can't stop them. Bullets won't work. You can't lock them up. Only Charlie can do it, and with our help he will.'

She turned and looked at Charlie. His face was serious and set in the way he had when he was determined about something. But it was more than that, she thought, he looked older, he looked a bit like the man he would become. With some discomfort she realised that he meant what he said, and for now any attempt at persuasion was likely to fall on deaf ears. She also knew that things were at work here that she couldn't even begin to understand. The creatures that had momentarily revealed themselves to her last night were beyond her worst imaginings – and whilst her rational brain was furiously trying to compartmentalize the whole experience into a box marked 'unexplained and best forgotten', in her heart she knew that this wasn't going away. Taking him home and carrying on as normal wasn't an option.

Charlie saw this thought process run its way across his mum's weary face. She had no idea how well he knew her and he suddenly felt a wave of love for her as he saw her making her decision. His mum was tough, and stubborn at times, she had needed to be when everything went pear-shaped for them after his dad disappeared, but she was also a realist. He could see that she had decided to stay and help, even before the words came out of her mouth.

'OK Charlie – for now – but you need something to eat.'

Chapter 14

The training was important to Bash. He hadn't seen Charlie in action last night, and whilst he was amazed by the intensity of the power that surged around him, so much stronger than he remembered it with Alex, he was still worried about what they were getting into. Although Mathilda was a little older than Charlie, they were still just children. He needed them both, but wished it was just him. He found himself torn between the contradiction of wanting to get them out of the way and knowing that ultimately he had to take them with him. The only answer was to get them as ready as he could. He was sure that time was short. The raid last night and the resulting death of the Nasties would prompt them into action. He didn't know much about the Nasties, but he did know they needed to feed to survive, and common sense dictated that after a defeat they would want to regroup and regain strength. As Charlie had said, more children would be taken.

Mathilda was a bit worried. She needed to call Aunt Val. She had told her that she was staying at a friend's house, a sleepover, and that was fine, but even though she knew she would be busy at the weekend, it would only take one call to Chloe's mum and the game would be up. Val never got up early on a Sunday so she probably had a bit of time yet, but nonetheless her anxiety twisted in her stomach. If only she had a phone like all her friends. She had asked for one once, but her aunt said she was on a budget and a phone for Mathilda was a luxury she couldn't afford. The flip side of this was the relentless excitement of what she had found herself caught up in. Yesterday had passed in a blur. The climactic attack on the house and the aftermath had already taken on the substance of some bizarre dream in her memory. And now the exciting prospect of being trained to fight the creatures. Her hands itched to grab her bow and start showing everyone what she could do. Since her parents died she had been a passenger, not just in this situation but in her own life, drifting through school and friendships like an interested observer, but feeling oddly disconnected from the living itself. Now she could do more – be more. It was odd that this situation made her feel more alive than she had done since her parents had died. She felt in control, like she had a purpose. One thing was for sure, she didn't want to miss out.

Bash called Charlie over and asked him to sit down next to him. The grass was heavy with dew, but he was untroubled by such things, and anyway no sooner had he sat down than he bounced back up again as he started to explain the basics of transferring the flame.

Mathilda watched carefully. She had relaxed after calling her aunt on Cathy's mobile. To her surprise she had been OK about Mathilda staying out a bit longer, she hadn't even asked her where she was, which was unlike her. She assumed her aunt was caught up in her own plans and that was fine. She watched Bash eagerly as he talked about the way they would make their weapons combine with Charlie's flames. Her hands gripped the bow tightly.

Cathy was less relaxed. She had agreed for Charlie to stay, but the more she listened to Bash the more she wished they could just get the hell out of there. On top of that she was frustrated by the fact she wouldn't be a participant in whatever adventure they thought they were going on. She understood that at the last moment she had been able to see at least a flicker of these Nasties, but before then she had been completely helpless. She would be a hindrance if they were fighting, but she was damned if her son was going to get into any danger without her by his side.

It was the moment of truth. Bash had talked about the way Alex had passed the flame to his axe, but now he needed Charlie to give it a try. If it didn't work then he was on his own, at least in terms of any real fighting.

Charlie could call up the flame into his hands and manipulate it with ease now, pulling the dazzling light into different shapes and forms. He felt like a magician – but instead of pulling a rabbit from a hat or a dove from his sleeve like those old-fashioned guys on the TV, he could produce blazing shards of flame. It was odd how it felt so natural too him after all the effort that had gone into his failed attempts yesterday. Even so he felt nervous as Bash held his axe in front of him and asked him to do as he said – to pass the flame.

In essence it all sounded so simple. His dad had just pushed the flame over and into the axe, but he was sure there was much more to it than that. The flame was strong when it was with him, but he noticed that its intensity diminished once he let it go. That was to be expected, he guessed, but somehow it made him less confident that he could make sure both Bash and Mathilda would have an effective and reliable weapon when they next ran into the Nasties. The last thing he wanted was for either of them to be left mid-battle with nothing to protect themselves. The nerves he was feeling were reflected in the flame he produced. It stuttered slightly in his hand, reminding him of the sound made by a camping stove in a breeze, a crackling roar as the flame tried to right itself. He was painfully aware of how little he knew about the ability he possessed and he vowed to find out more when he had the time. He would find the other keepers of the flame that Bash had mentioned, the ones who were missing. They could help him fill in all the gaps in the story so he could really understand what a Watcher was and what he could do.

He concentrated, trying hard to shed his nerves and just enjoy the feeling of power that flowed through him. It was clear that being relaxed was the key; as soon as he tensed up or got scared the power found it more difficult to negotiate its path from wherever it was born within him out to his hands. But it was hard not to be nervous with so much at stake.

Bash had wandered over to the house and returned carrying his axe. He held it out in front of him, both hands clasped around the broad handle, blade facing forward towards where he stood.

'If we can get this up and running we're in business,' he said in a light-hearted voice, but Charlie could see from his eyes that he was serious. 'Just do what we have been talking about. You can do this.'

Charlie closed his eyes and put his hands on the blade of the axe. He took a deep breath and tried to do what Bash had said. The flame rolled down and around his hands, blazing brightly onto the blade of the axe, dripping to the floor at his feet. He pushed out with his mind, doing more than just throwing the flame away like he had been doing. This was different. It required him to push it away as a living thing, something that would endure after its immediate connection with him was gone. The feeling was very different to when he simply fired flame at things. He could feel his hands and shoulders shaking as he concentrated, his brow furrowed and mouth pursed as he tried to keep control of the energy he was channelling into the axe. Bash watched carefully, feeling the vibration of the transferred energy radiating from the axe down his own arms. 'It's working, Charlie, keep going,' he said.

Charlie's arms were hurting now and he could feel a bubble of pressure building up in his head. Thin beads of sweat were forming on his brow and his mum moved towards him anxiously, her hands reaching out to grab him.

'No, Cathy,' shouted Bash. 'Leave him alone, he needs to finish this.' She paused, torn between helping him and the harsh anxiety she heard in his voice.

It was so hard, Charlie thought. He could see what was required. The flame he was transferring had to be fuelled from him. He needed to be its constant source of energy. This meant he had to push part of himself into the weapon. It hurt to do it and he felt himself teetering on the edge of consciousness, his mind drifting softly away from him. As his legs buckled under him he heard the echoing sound of his mum calling his name; the link between the flame and Bash's axe was clear in his mind, the power disconnecting from him to it with an audible snap, before he was plunged into darkness.

Sunlight flickering across his eyelids and the gentle sound of his mum's voice greeted him as he slowly came round. The face of Mum and Mathilda wavered into focus in front of him, and he rubbed the back of his hand furiously across his face as he pushed himself up onto his elbows. 'Oh, Charlie, love, don't get up too quickly. Thank goodness you're OK,' his mum said at once, her face pale and anxious.

Over her shoulder he could see Bash and Mathilda staring down at him with some concern but also something more – was it excitement? Bash looked at him with a smile before raising his hand to reveal the brilliantly bright blue glow of his axe. His grin broadened as he casually waved the axe back and forth, drawing a vivid trace of blue in the air behind it. Mathilda's face pushed in eagerly. 'Can you do that for me as well, Charlie?' she said.

Chapter 15

The school playground was emptying out fast as parents scurried back and forth to collect their children. Teachers maintained a watchful eye and carefully ticked off the name of each child when they were picked up. The early summer heat had faded and the breeze was cool and damp with the promise of rain. The trees that surrounded the concrete play area swayed in the stuttering wind, leaves rustling secretly as a slightly hunched figure carefully emptied the bins that dotted the playing field. Mr. Carmichael had been caretaker at the school for as long as anyone could remember. A constant presence, barely changed in thirty years, almost as if he had been born with greying hair and a wizened and weather-worn face. He grimaced with distaste as his foot slid in a dark slurry of muck underneath the trees. He cursed the errant dog-owner who had carelessly allowed its mutt to foul in the school playing field. Did these people not even consider that children ran around across this grass? 'Bloody dogs,' he muttered. He would have them all shot if he could. He preferred his beloved Persian cat and couldn't think for the life of him why anyone would entertain an animal as stupid as a dog.

He dragged his left foot over the grass, wiping the worst of the thick sludge away, his nose wrinkling in expectation of the usual foul smell. There was a smell but rather different than he expected, bitter and metallic, but horribly familiar. Wiping his glasses carefully with a handkerchief he stowed in the top pocket of his overalls, Mr. Carmichael peered more closely at the thick pool of black sludge that was splattered amongst the grasses that grew tall up to the tree-lined fence. Whatever it was, it wasn't dog mess. He looked closer and could see that the sludge was rippling slightly, flowing against all expectations back up the long grass stems and pooling at the top in peculiar clumps. As he watched, one of these clumps quivered and with an audible 'plink' rose up and into the trees above. He rubbed at his eyes, and moved further under the branches, a shadow now amongst the darker ones that surrounded him. He looked up into the leaves above him, unsure what to make of it all, his brow furrowed.

In the tree above the Beleth perched. In its grasp lay the limp body of someone Mr. Carmichael would have recognised at once if only his befuddled senses could see through the psychological fog that shrouded the Nasties from view. Alfie Brewer had been a thorn in the side of the staff at Therwick's three junior schools and had caused him no end of trouble with his constant petty acts of vandalism. Shipped from one school to the next after second and third chances had been neglected by him and his frankly useless parents, Alfie had continued on his seemingly inevitable trajectory towards disaster. It was fair to say, however, that the end of his short and troubled life was not quite what anyone might have predicted. The Nasties had been desperate for food and his shifty presence in the fields at break time as he tried to pull himself over the chain link fence had been too good an opportunity to miss. The chance was taken, Beleth had swept him up and away before he had even had time to scream. It desperately needed to feed and so despite itself had remained in situ for the last three hours absorbing the final flickering remnants of Alfie Brewer's life, sating its hunger and preparing for the birth of more siblings it would use to crush the boy who had surprised them all with his powers.

The old man below him stared up into the tree, and Beleth toyed with the idea of dropping down and finishing him off as well, its anger at the stupid sheep-like face that looked up at it making it bristle. The husk of Alfie broke up like dust in its claws, blowing gently away on the breeze. It knew it was not the time for such things. Another dead fool would just make it harder for it to feed again on what it really needed. Old humans were bearable if required but they didn't deliver anything like the power contained within a child. Besides, it knew from its feast that Alfie wouldn't be missed for some time yet. When it ate his essence (what the humans might call his soul), it had captured all there was to know of Alfie's sad life. A flicker of empty rooms, peeling wallpaper and the ghostly shapes of disinterested parents cast in the glow of a TV screen. Not that it cared about this. The pain it had tasted in the boy's soul made its feast all the sweeter, but his absence, so typical and expected, meant that the scant precautions the adults had thrown up since the feeding had begun would be no worse for a while longer. Alfie's parents weren't going to report him missing.

It hissed softly down at the old man, a sound he couldn't hear, but almost certainly felt as his face turned pale with fright causing him to stumble backwards away from the shadows of the trees. In a moment it whirled itself away through the dimensions that rippled alongside the world, reappearing in the cellar of the old house where it crouched hunched and silent in the corner away from the growing horde. With eyes closed and breathing slowing, it turned itself to the task of spawning. After that, more feeding, before battle would commence. In the darkness the Nasties hissed in delight at the prospect.

The Beleth had not underestimated the vigilance of Alfie Brewers parents. When he didn't come into school the next day the head teacher had called his parents immediately and insisted that they accompany Alfie to school unless they had a note from the doctors to say he was too ill to attend. Mrs. Brewer, a scrawny and dishevelled looking woman, had said Alfie was asleep upstairs and couldn't be woken. She had tried, she said, but he wouldn't get up and what was she meant to do about that? None of them understood what it was like to be a mum to a kid like Alfie. In truth she hadn't even looked in Alfie's room, the closest she had come to it was when she weaved past it late yesterday evening in search of Bob's cigarettes which he had sent her to collect lest he miss any of the football. She didn't understand Alfie or any of the other children she had brought into the world. Alfie was the youngest and a mistake. The others had all gone off to do whatever they did, she saw them infrequently and cared even less about what they were up to, as long as it didn't require any money or effort from her. Alfie, however, was a pain, phone calls from teachers and visits from the police interrupting her plans and making life complicated. Bob couldn't stand him either. So when the clearly exasperated head teacher was off the phone and she wavered uncertainly at the foot of the stairs, wondering if she should at least check the box room where no doubt the lazy little sod would be skulking, she did what she always did. She wandered to the fridge and got herself and Bob another drink.

Chapter 16

The arrow, encased in its blue flame, quivered against the tension of the bow string, the soft whistle of the breeze reverberating against it as Mathilda held it steady. To begin with the blaze had been very distracting, her hands instinctively tense at the prospect of grasping an arrow that seemed covered in flame, anticipating a burn that didn't come, but after a few hiccups her aim had returned. Staring straight down the line of the arrow, she stood firm in the long grass of Bash's garden waiting for the targets to reveal themselves. Her face was calm, her breathing steady despite the accelerated beat of her heart. The trouble was this was almost too much fun, she thought to herself. It was hard to associate the thrill of the training with the real danger to come. But the relative safety of Bash's garden and his mock targets couldn't continue. They knew that. The rumour of another missing boy had focused their minds, bringing them back to the task in hand, when in truth they had all fallen into the dangerous game of assuming they had plenty of time. It was too easy to get lulled into the ritual of training and talking, pushing the inevitable further down the road.

Out of the corner of her eye she saw a flicker of blackness as a shape swept up and out from the trees. In a fluid motion she rotated her hips and released the arrow in a streak of blue directly at the target, piercing it through the centre and sending it crashing to the floor. At the same time a further target dropped down behind her, causing her to roll instinctively over to her side, coming up with an arrow miraculously drawn and ready to fire. Bash watched her with a grim smile of admiration. She was so fast, he thought, and the training regime had made her faster still. But shooting at old bits of tarpaulin on ropes was not the same thing as a horde of slavering Nasties intent on death. He knew that the time would come when the skills they were honing were put to the ultimate test. If the boy from school had been taken that meant the Nasties would be gathering, building numbers and strength. He knew they couldn't afford to wait much longer or the number might be too great. He couldn't contemplate another scene like the one he had faced in Italy all those years ago – not with just three of them in the fight.

'Right, let's call it a night, shall we?' he said, clapping his hands together encouragingly. 'Well done. So quick, Mathilda, and you, Charlie – wow, what can I say, brilliant.'

Charlie smiled and gave his mum a high five as he walked back into the kitchen at the back of the house. Cathy gathered up her car keys and picked up Mathilda's hockey bag into which she had carefully placed the bow and quiver of arrows. She still couldn't get used to handling the flaming quiver of arrows, and tentatively picked at the shoulder strap which was mercifully free of flame.

'What next, Bash?' asked Charlie, looking back over his shoulder as they filed down the hall to the front door.

'Well you get a good night's rest and we catch up again tomorrow after school,' he replied, smiling as Charlie and Mathilda ran across the drive to secure the front seat, a race Mathilda won this time much to Charlie's disgust.

'So what is next, Bash – really?' asked Cathy. She looked at him carefully. She had heard the rumours about poor Alfie Brewer. Her friend at work, whose cousin was a policeman, had said that it was only a matter of time before they checked his house. Two days was a long time for a kid to be missing in Therwick these days. Alfie's parents had denied access to a doctor yesterday, sent there on the insistence of Alfie's school. The police would put an end to the mystery tomorrow, her friend had said. Maybe they would find those other kids in there, she had said, before quickly apologising for suggesting such a thing. Cathy had said little. They wouldn't be finding the other kids there, that was for sure, but she fervently hoped that they would find Alfie safe and well.

Bash looked at her, wanting to say something comforting. 'We have a little more time, I think. I need to think this through, I will have it all sorted in the next week or so. I've got a couple of ideas. In the meantime we keep them safe and happy – right?'

'A week?' Cathy replied. 'OK, but you need to tell me what you're planning. If you think I am going to let you run off with Charlie and Mathilda without me knowing what is going on, you're way off. They think it's just a video game or something at the moment, you know that, don't you?'

'I know, Cath,' replied Bash with a pained expression. 'But we have a bit of time – trust me.'

In reality time was running out. A hasty glance into a collapsed cellar of a certain old house would have put paid to the idea of waiting a week (or maybe two).

The Nasties were gathering in strength and numbers. The earthen floor writhed with twisted shapes of all sizes, squirming over and around each other, occasionally hissing in anger. In the corner Beleth squatted, the flesh on its back boiling like tar, blisters forming that swelled and burst, spewing forth another to join the legion.

It shuddered, the energy it had drained from the child spent, but the mewling newcomers that hissed and spat at each other around its massive clawed feet were ample reward. Its eyes split open across its vast head, a dozen now opening in a crescent, deep red and blinking together slowly in the darkness. It saw the legion it had formed, over a hundred strong and hungry, so very hungry. It could feel their appetite; it could feel everything they were as an extension of its own mind and body. Even now they combed the woods surrounding the old house, devouring everything they came across. The woods were silent now, the local wildlife either eaten or driven away by the insatiable hunger of the gathering horde. Beleth rose up to its full height, its smaller kin mewling and squealing at its feet. They were one and the time had come to destroy the boy, the last of the Watchers, after which they could feed.

Humans were just sheep after all, and they would cull without mercy.

Chapter 17

The cub camp had been held on the fringes of Therwick woods for nearly fifteen years. The site had been there so long, the ground where the campfire was built was so scorched that even in the summer months the grass refused to grow. Archibald Deacon sat comfortably on an old tree stump that formed part of the circle that surrounded the fire. With practised movements he carefully turned the marshmallows that were softly blackening over the flames that licked up into the dusk. The kids expected him to do this, and the parents liked it too, harking back as it did to older times when life was simpler. But that was the whole point of the cub scouts for him, getting the kids to do old-fashioned stuff, away from the endless reach of video games, Snapchat, YouTube and all the other stuff he didn't like or understand. He had being doing it himself for fifty years, ever since his own dad had taken him down to the crumbling cub hut on the local park, where as a ten-year-old boy he had found a place to belong.

Fortunately there were still a good number of boys and girls who liked building a camp or lighting a fire, although tonight and indeed for the last three to four weeks, numbers had dwindled as concerned parents had decided they didn't want their kids out and about. He had been slightly put out by this at first, but understood. The horrific loss of three local children in such a short space of time was too big a deal to be ignored. As diligent as ever, he had spoken with the police and also held a meeting in the much newer scout hut that sat in the park (a reflection of his own fundraising efforts over the last ten years), where he had addressed the concerns of parents and guardians. To coin a phrase – he was prepared.

So tonight with the help of three willing and, he reflected, overprotective parents he was confident that the overnight camp would be a success. There was still time for a story or two before the one of the children would be entrusted with tamping down the fire and they would retire to their tents for the night. He would stay up a while longer. On the recommendation of the young police constable he had spoken with he had decided that some form of night watch would be in order, and each of the three tents had an adult in occupation. He had even devised a few early warning systems and the kids had enjoyed setting them up on the premise of providing advance notice if any deer or foxes wandered into camp. The parents had looked less convinced, smiling uncomfortably as he had explained how the tripwires and noisemakers would work, the unspoken truth of their purpose heavy in the air, but in the end they had all set about enthusiastically putting together the system he had devised. He was pleased with it in a way only a scout of forty years' experience could be.

The evening sky was thickening towards dark and, as the last of the marshmallows were slurped up by the children, Archibald decided it was time to call it a night. He already had in mind who should dampen the fire. James was the smallest in the group, quiet and reserved. When being picked up or dropped off, his mother always hovered uncertainly around him like a moth circling a light, but she had, against all expectations, allowed him to come on the camp with his dad, and so it was only right he got the chance to deal with the fire.

Archibald noted the quiet efficiency in which the flame was dampened, and he patted James on the back as he led him over to his tent. The other children were getting themselves ready, lamps being lit, creating dancing shadows against the heavy canvas. Gradually the lamps within the three tents were turned down and the snatches of conversation and laughter grew more muffled. He was tired but looked forward to sitting in peace for a spell before he retired to his tent. He thought he would stay awake for a while yet, but with the fire out he could feel the drop in temperature and shivered despite the warmth of the evening. It seemed impossible to him that such evil could have settled on Therwick, where he had lived all his life without ever seeing anything that would prevent him from encouraging youngsters to get out and enjoy all the freedom the woods offered. It was only a matter of time before kids didn't even step out of the door, he thought, instead locking themselves away endlessly attached to screens. He sighed heavily at the thought, looking up as a light wind started to blow softly through the treetops.

In the woods above Therwick, the Nasties were rising. The time for secrecy had passed. They aimed to take the boy and whatever else they came across. As one they poured forth from the cellar of the old house, the darkness they carried with them sweeping across the ground as they darted across the woodland floor, leaping from tree to tree in ever increasing numbers, appearing and disappearing as they whirled between the world and the dark places between. Beleth watched approvingly as its horde poured down the hill like a wave of tar. With a massive flex of its muscles it launched itself into the sky, spinning into nothingness as it projected forward to the front of the horde. A few miles ahead the twinkling lights of Therwick could be seen through the trees. The Nasties screamed in delight and quickened the pace.

Archibald awoke with a start. He had dropped off, although quite when and for how long he was not sure. Disoriented, he struggled to pull up his sleeve and check his watch, wincing as his back stiffened from the awkward position he had slept in his old camping chair. He rubbed his hand across his eyes, blinking furiously, but was unable to pick out the dial on his watch. The tents around him were quiet, with only a soft snoring sound drifting across from the one pitched closest to the fire. Archibald relaxed back into the chair, which creaked as he shifted his weight back into the rickety frame. He needed to go to his tent and sleep properly. His back would probably seize up for a month if he didn't lie flat for the next few hours. His tent was pitched at the back of the clearing and he reached into his pocket for his mini torch, the light carefully wrapped in red muslin to dampen the brightness of the light and prevent his night vision from being lost. Such small details continued to delight him and he smiled to himself as he rocked forward to ease himself up. As he did so he heard the first faint murmurings of a noise, soft at first like the distant roar of waves on a shore, but growing in intensity, within a heartbeat loud enough for him to hear the crack and frantic rustle of foliage above and to his right in the trees.

Archibald didn't see the attack. The furthest tent suddenly ripped itself free from its tethered mooring, flapping up into the air in a twist of shredded nylon, its occupants making a strangled cry of alarm before the wave of Nasties tore them apart. The force of impact on the next tent sent Archibald's own old canvas relic flying towards him in a bundle of ropes and twisted material. The weight of the canvas knocked him to the floor, where he lay gasping for breath under its folds. Around him the Nasties attacked, screams now echoing around the clearing as the remaining tents were torn open. In the darkness parents were separated from children and swiftly dispatched. The Nasties killed the grown-ups with a chilling efficiency, wasting no time and leaving the corpses aside, seeking out the sweeter flesh of the children. They swarmed in greater numbers over them, like ants on a crippled bug, biting and tearing, frantically taking all the vitality they could before Beleth took hold and claimed the prize. Within minutes seven of the eight children in the camp were dead, the last vestiges of their lives shimmering away in the frantic scrabbling of the horde of Nasties.

Only James survived. He stood cowering amid a circle of Nasties, too shocked to even see or understand the carnage around him. It was surely a dream, he thought, tears streaming down his face as the circle broke and Beleth stepped forward towering above him. It stared down at James, eyes opening one after the other, red and terrible, mouth splitting into an endless grin of teeth. 'Just a dream...wake up soon,' James whispered as its jaws closed swiftly over him and he was choked back, sliced and swallowed, just conscious enough to feel a final horrifying blast of indescribable pain before nothingness. The Nasties howled to the sky in joyful unison.

Underneath his canvas tomb, Archibald whimpered, his heart beating so loudly he thought it might burst. Inhuman screams sounded around him and he felt his bladder give way, tears springing from his eyes as he sobbed soundlessly in utter terror. Slowly the noise faded, claws scrabbled over and around him but becoming distant before he was left in silence, the only sound his shrill breath rasping against the rough canvas of his tent. By inches he moved himself carefully out into the clearing, eyes desperately searching for a sign of life. The smell of blood assaulted his nostrils, coppery and metallic and as he groped forward his hand slipped in a slick of gore that had once been James's dad. Archibald Deacon began to scream.

Chapter 18

Charlie was sleeping fitfully. Cathy could hear the soft creak and squeal of his mattress as he tossed and turned in his bedroom. It had been a difficult journey back from Bash's house. She had felt cruel cutting short Charlie and Mathilda's excited chatter in the back of the car, but it was all getting too much for her. They seemed to think it was some great big game. When they talked of attacking the Nasties, it was like they were starring in a film or something, like it was a forgone conclusion it would all turn out OK and the heroes would head off into the sunset.

But they weren't heroes, they were kids under the supervision of an ex-drunk and local weirdo, someone who had burst in and out of her life years ago, stained forever by the disappearance of her husband and the crazed explanations that followed. Despite the madness of the attack at Bash's house a few weeks ago, and the fragile acknowledgment from her that the mad stories her husband had told her might be true after all, she couldn't put Charlie at risk any longer. She would go to the police in the morning. Put this in the hands of the professionals. Sipping her glass of wine carefully, she couldn't quite believe she hadn't done that already.

Chapter 19

Across Therwick the lights were going out. If you could have flown over the town and looked down at that moment, you would have observed what looked like a wave of blackness spreading east from the woods. It moved slowly at first, heading up the main road, to all the world looking as if a blanket of darkness was being rolled out over the road into the town, street lamps blinking out one by one. Look closer and the source of this wave of night was clearer.

Zigzagging back and forth, leaping from shadow to shadow the Nasties came, smashing street lamps along the way. A dog barked briefly into the night as the scampering claws raced closer, but swiftly silenced itself when the creatures passed nearby, its instincts strangled by a crushing wave of terror that left it whimpering and confused. Within minutes the Nasties had reached the railway bridge that served as an entrance to the residential area of the town.

At the head of the wave, Beleth paused. It could sense the beating heart of the boy, now only streets away. Through its red eyes, it could distinguish the faint blue glow given off by the last Watcher, drifting on the air around his home, a beacon on which the horde could focus. There were so many now, blood-hungry and frantic after the carnage at the camp site in the woods. Although they hadn't encountered any other humans in the surge towards the boy, it could sense the frenzied desire to smash and ravage the sleeping humans nested in the houses that lined the quiet streets. The boy was the prize. After he had been taken they could feed all they wanted. These thoughts passed out into the hive mind of the horde, restraining them, holding them back from the carnage they so desperately wanted.

Cathy felt the air in the house change. From warm and stuffy to cold in a heartbeat. It woke her up, her head more than a little fuzzy from the wine she had drunk a few hours ago. Her eyes were open but the dark was so dense that she poked herself painfully in one eye as she raised her hands to her face. There was also a smell, thick and fetid. As she sprang up out of bed she knew they had come for him.

Charlie was having a dream. In it his dad was running from him, a distant shadow racing ahead, always in sight but never close enough for him to touch. He was running through a tunnel, towards a pinprick of light. His dad was ahead, racing towards that light as well. It felt like they had been running for days. When he tried to call out to him, to ask him to stop, the words were rendered silent as they left his lips. His dad ran on. Sobbing with frustration he ran too, his legs feeling weaker and weaker, the ground beneath his feet sucking at his toes, making it harder for him to carry on. In his dream he stumbled and went to his knees, sinking immediately into a thick black syrup. He looked up, screaming again for his dad to stop. Way up ahead now, he could see that at last his dad was standing still. He turned back towards him and for the first time he could see his face clearly. In his dream tears sprang to his eyes and he called out again. His dad was beckoning him forward and he was starting to make out his words, softly but getting louder as he got closer. 'Wake up, Charlie, wake up, Charlie, wake up, Charlie,' endlessly over and over.

He woke with a gasp, his body shrouded in flickering blue flame. The darkness in his room was a solid thing, with nothing to be seen beyond the flame that enveloped him. He threw back his covers and sat up reaching out in front of him blindly, disorientated by the darkness. The flames around him spluttered, the edges tattering and blinking out into the darkness like embers rising from a bonfire. He called the flame forward, brightening the immediate space around his body but still unable to penetrate the wider blackness. 'Muummm,' he called. The sound of his voice was muffled, flat and without strength. He stumbled to his feet, silently cursing that his own bedroom had turned into an unfamiliar obstacle course, but welcoming at least the familiar reality offered by the edge of his bookshelf as it cracked into his thigh. Hands flailing in front of him located the door frame and eventually the door handle.

'Mum,' he called again. 'Where are you?' He pulled the door open onto what should have been the landing.

It took a moment or two to make sense of what lay before him. The swirling vortex of black in front of him funnelled down through what should have been the wall next to the bathroom. Terror spiked him, fuelling a rush of adrenalin that set his heart racing. The blue flames swelled around him.

'Mum, where are you?' he called, stepping gingerly out into the darkness. The floor was still there, his foot making welcome contact despite the fact that his eyes could see nothing. A roaring sound filled his ears, a white noise of static, blotting out all normal sound and further disorientating him. Faintly and to his left or right, he could no longer tell, he thought he could hear his mum calling him. 'Charlieeeee.'

Instinctively he raised the flame from his hands, effortlessly forming a spear of brilliant light. The darkness in front of him thickened. He recoiled as a flurry of motion pushed against the blackness, shapes forming and scrabbling against reality. In an instant they were through, ripping the darkness to one side, tattered threads bursting out, as a dozen Nasties poured through the inter dimensional gap.

He had little time to react, the flame spearing the first of them, exploding into its open jaws, its kin scrabbling over and through its dying body to get to him. He cried out as they clawed towards him. He had so little room to manoeuvre with his back pushed against the wall. The flames around him swelled, searing the claws that grabbed at him, burning talons to ashes and causing the Nasties to fall back, howling and spitting. He moved to his left, pushing along with the wall at his back, its cold reality grounding him and giving him a point of reference despite the chaos around him. Mum's room was only a few feet away, he told himself—he just needed to keep moving. More Nasties came, wrenching themselves through the vortex that continued to wheel and turn in the space that was once his house. There were so many, if only Bash and Mathilda could be here to help, he thought.

The Nasties edged towards him, a wall of teeth and thrashing claws, matching his every step back. The flames continued to swell around him, the blue light reflected back in the distorted red and black eyes of those nearest to him. He felt the door to his mum's bedroom behind him, the doorknob jabbing him in his back.

Whilst maintaining the barrier of flame he was projecting in front of him, his left hand desperately scrambled at the knob behind his back. The Nasties inched closer, sensing his panic. The tear in reality behind the gathering horde widened with an audible rip. A huge hand, thick with talons, tore open its tattered edge.

He watched in horror as Beleth pulled itself through, turning its massive head left and right before focusing its myriad red eyes on him. Its face broke into an approximation of a grin, the crescent of teeth dripping viscous saliva. The horde paused, separating to create a path for it through the throng. They waited eagerly for the signal to attack. The doorknob was slick in his hand; the bloody thing was always difficult to open, he thought incoherently, his hand wresting back and forth as he looked into the endless eyes of the Beleth.

Bash was staring at a bottle of whisky that he had found in the garage. He had discovered it by accident. He had been sure that the last of the booze had been thrown out on the day he decided to help Charlie. But there it was, the bottle a bit dusty and discoloured but its reassuring amber contents intact. The seal at the lid was untouched. He stared, while his mind ran over and over, the same old thoughts. *Just one*, it said, *just one nip and then you can throw it away, or if not throw away, you can put it back in the garage, for another time, out of sight. No problem, you can do it – no problem.*

He rubbed his hands over his face, hearing the soft scratch of stubble in the silent room. It was such a small thing, but at the same time enormous. He knew in his heart that there was no such thing as one drink. The roaring confidence and bewitching pleasure that would consume his brain moments after the liquid created hot fire in his stomach would open him up again. There would be no stopping him. But at the same time, a sneaky and peevish part of him whined and whispered in his ear. He deserved a drink, it said, after all he had been through, and blimey, one drink wasn't going to kill anyone, was it? Charlie was fine, safe and sound, he had been working so hard and needed a break from all this madness, wasn't really his problem in the first place, who could blame him, no-one, no-one at all. On and on the thoughts spiralled.

With a force of will he pulled himself up from his chair. He walked stiffly, on borrowed legs, to the kitchen. He splashed cold water from the tap over his face, welcoming the slap it provided to his senses. Distracted, he reached over and flicked on the radio, anything to take his mind off the thought of a drink.

The speakers spat out a blaze of static, swelling up and down across the dial. What was going on – some sort of interference? It was not stormy, no high winds, no reason for this, but all the same the radio stubbornly refused to catch a station.

All at once he felt bad. Something was wrong, he knew it in his bones.

He moved quickly back to the front room, his hip knocking heavily against the doorframe, causing him to pull back his lips in a wince. The bottle of whisky was forgotten, his eyes fixed immediately on the bright blue glow of his axe, leant against the side of his chair. A warning sign. He needed to speak to Cathy, to check that Charlie was OK, that they were both OK. His mobile phone was on the kitchen table with his keys. Cathy had insisted that he get it up and running again, pushing the money into his hand so he could buy a top up and put some fuel in his battered old car. He flicked to his contacts and scrolled quickly down to Cathy Picker. The ring tone repeated over and again in his ear. *Answer the phone, Cath*, he thought, *please.*

Cathy was pulling desperately on the bedroom door handle. Beyond it she could only hear a deep and terrifying roar of static and faintly, oh so faintly, what sounded like Charlie calling for her help. She'd pulled and twisted at the door handle with all her strength, her bare foot planted in the middle of the door as she leant back and screamed. Behind her, on the bedside table amongst the scattered bits of jewellery, her phone lit up, buzzing and vibrating its way towards the edge. The sound of the ringtone, a jaunty tune wholly out of place, shocked her out of her desperate battle with the door. She looked longingly at the phone as she continued to heave at the door. Muscles in her back rippled and wavered. Suddenly the door flew open and in a flash of blue light Charlie fell back and on top of her. Flames roared from his outstretched palms, and beyond them she could see a wall of blackness.

'Charlie,' she screamed, wrapping her arms around him.

Charlie looked back over his shoulder and she could see the tears of pain streaming down his face. 'Mum, I can't hold on,' he cried. 'I'm sorry.'

Out of the blackness a huge muscled arm formed, flowing down into a hand shimmering with spikes and claws. It grasped Charlie by the foot, its flesh hissing and steaming as it broke through the wavering flames that encased his body. He looked desperately into his mum's eyes, a plea for help forming at his lips before he was wrenched from her grasp and submerged into the blackness beyond the door. In a heartbeat the static roar stopped and the darkness swirled away, leaving her on her back, the only sound the tinny ringtone braying out its tune in accompaniment to its final journey to the edge of the table. It dropped to the floor, the tone muffled and then silenced as whoever was calling gave up.

Chapter 20

Mathilda was woken by frantic banging on the front door and the sound of footsteps across the hall. With one eye open, she hauled herself out of bed, the last remnants of sleep leaving her as she heard her aunt's strident voice.

'Who on earth are you?' she cried. 'No, she is in bed asleep, do you have any idea what time it is?'

She quickly wrapped her old faded dressing gown around herself and ran across the landing to the top of the stairs. Bash and Cathy looked up at her from the porch. 'He's gone,' Cathy managed to say, 'They took him,' before her face collapsed into tears.

Aunt Val was completely at a loss. The lady, Cathy something or another, was inconsolable. Even the fabled powers of sweet tea and stoic reassurance failed to help. Mathilda said she was a good friend of the woman's son, but he had gone off somewhere and that seemed to be the source of all the fuss. Quite understandable at this moment in time, but how Mathilda fitted into this she didn't know. They were an odd lot and with the recent events in Therwick she was more than a little concerned about what Mathilda had got mixed up in. Her suggestion that they call the police had been met with such a clear look of derision from the man that she hadn't dared to offer any further suggestions.

The man, who to her eye looked more than a little unhinged, sat next to the woman, desperate to comfort her but clearly not knowing how. When Val had offered Cathy a glass of sherry, truly the last weapon in her social armoury, the man had focused on the bottle with a look of such fierce intensity she had been worried the bottle would grow hot and shatter in her hand. The bottle had been taken from her with indecent haste by Mathilda, who had quickly suggested she try to find Cathy a blanket to help with her the shaking. She agreed that might help and with no small amount of relief had headed upstairs to find something suitable. When she had gone Bash turned quickly to Mathilda and filled her in on what had happened.

'So I arrived at Charlie's house and knocked for what seemed like a lifetime, I must have woke up half the street. Dogs were barking all over town. It was chaos. I had to force open the door. The Nasties had come. They took Charlie—he's gone.'

Mathilda thought quickly. 'So where do we think they took him? Can we work out a way to find him? Think, Bash—was there anything that Charlie's dad showed you that might help us?'

He tried to think. He felt so helpless. He cursed himself, hitting his fist down hard on his leg in frustration. What use was he? he thought, gritting his teeth. What a joke – Pete Bashir, saviour of nothing and no-one. All that messing around, pretending they were preparing, training and they had just come and taken Charlie. Easy as that. How could he have got it so wrong? He stared into space, thoughts racing. His eyes were drawn to the rucksack he had set down by the door of the stairs. He had stuffed his axe into it before leaping into his car and driving to Cathy's house, its fierce glow piercing the stitching as it lay in the passenger seat, only dimming shortly after he turned into Charlie's street.

'My axe,' he said suddenly, making Cathy jump. 'It knows when the Nasties are near – the flames react to them. Maybe we can use it to locate them, to find out where they took Charlie.'

Mathilda was nodding in agreement, the idea forming in her mind. 'I have my bow too. Between us maybe we can home in on him, you know, like a compass. It's got to be worth a try.'

He got to his feet and grabbed the old rucksack, pulling the axe out and holding it in front of him. To his frustration it refused to offer up any secrets, it was just an axe. It refused to glow or give them any clues. Bash spat out his words in frustration. 'They could be anywhere. God, where do we start, I can't wander around Therwick waiting for this thing to start glowing.'

Mathilda heard her aunt coming back down the stairs. 'Put that away – quick,' she hissed.

Aunt Val looked uncertainly at Bash's flushed face and gritted teeth. 'I have a nice blanket,' she said, offering it to Cathy. 'Are you all OK?' she ventured. Cathy, who by now had some colour back in her face, thanked her and pulled the old cotton sheet tightly around her.

'Thank you, Valerie, you've been very kind. I feel a bit better now.'

Seeing an opportunity to restore order and normality, Val once again suggested a call to the police.

'Given what's been happening I am sure they will want to help you, even if your boy has just popped round a friend's house and not told you—you know, like boys do,' she said.

Cathy mustered up a smile and asked for another cup of tea, holding her cup out to her. Aunt Val took hold of the normal social cue with the happy acceptance of someone diving back into a warm bed. From the kitchen they heard the soft rattle of cutlery and a radio being switched on. Bash looked at Cathy and gently took her hand. 'Do you have any ideas, Cathy? Did you see anything?' She shuddered slightly under the tightly wrapped sheet. 'No all I saw was blackness, nothing that can help us, what are we going to do?' she whispered as her voice tightened and tears began to flow again. A crash from the kitchen made them all jump.

'Auntie Val,' shouted Mathilda. 'Are you alright?'

She rushed back into the room, her face pale. 'Oh it's horrible,' she said. 'There's been an attack, at the scout camp out in Therwick woods. The man on the radio says there's been a massacre.'

Bash looked at her. 'The woods...' he said, his voice trailing off as his mind started working. *Of course*, he thought, *it all started there*. There was always a nest, somewhere for the Nasties to gather and grow. Therwick woods was the place to start.

Chapter 21

Mathilda wasn't sure how she would ever be able to explain any of this to Aunt Val, or to the police if she made good on her threat to call them unless they told her what was going on. Cathy and Bash had both tried to calm her down but when she had come back downstairs stuffing her bow into her hockey bag that was the final straw. They had ended up just leaving her, throwing apologies over their shoulders as they ran to Cathy's car.

Bash was right though, the attacks and disappearances were focused around Therwick woods. The young boy whose horse had been found, the little girl who lived so close to them, and now the scout camp and the undetermined number of children who had been hurt. Either way it all suggested that they needed to start there. Besides, they had no better ideas. Getting Cathy to wait at home was another matter. Bash pleaded with her, but she wasn't listening. It was her son, she said, and if they were going to try to find him then she was going to be right with them to the end. Bash had relented. They didn't have time to argue anymore. If they were to have any chance of finding Charlie alive they needed to act now.

The local radio station made it clear that accessing Therwick woods wasn't going to be easy. That whole side of town was cordoned off. The local police and their national counterparts were desperately trying to secure the crime scene and hold the press at bay. The scout leader had been found and by all accounts had suffered some sort of breakdown—shouting about demons coming out of the trees. The police had bundled him into the back of an ambulance to the dazzling accompaniment of a myriad camera flashes, ensuring his crazed face would be splashed all over the front pages of the newspapers the next day.

There were other ways into Therwick woods. The unmade roads, that allowed the forestry commission to rumble their big trucks in and out to fell trees, crisscrossed the area. Bash was familiar with these from his days when he would sometimes agree to buy the odd piece of timber for a job he was doing, and so it didn't take long for him to direct Cathy to a side road that looped around the police line that protected the shattered scout camp.

The sun was shining fitfully as they pulled up at the side of the track, and dust rising lazily in the air and dancing away on hidden breezes formed amongst the tightly packed trees that stretched away around them. They opened the car doors and stepped out into a pregnant stillness. Crickets chirped in the long grass that grew in the avenues of light amongst the trees but otherwise the woods were silent and brooding.

'I don't like it here,' said Mathilda without really thinking. 'It feels wrong.' Bash knew what she meant. The woods looked fine, beautiful even, but there was something behind the normality of it all. A creeping feeling that made the hairs on his arms stand up and his stomach churn. He reached into his backpack and pulled out his axe. It glowed a dull blue. It seemed the theory was working. They were on the right track.

Holding it out in front of him, with both hands clenched around its comforting solidness he turned in a slow circle watching for any change in the intensity of the glow. Sure enough as he circled to his right the blade grew brighter. They all stared at the axe with a mixture of fear and relief.

'I guess we head that way then,' he said.

Chapter 22

Charlie didn't know where he was, which way was up, down, left or right. There was only blackness. A throbbing blackness that pulsed in time with his heartbeat.

His senses were shut down. He couldn't feel his body, nor hear or smell anything. All that remained were his thoughts and the beat of his heart. He floated, embryonic, in the sanctuary of the dark. He didn't know how long he had been here, or where here actually was, but he felt safe, sleepy and dreamlike.

Time passed.

How had he got here? he wondered. *Am I dreaming?* The pulse of the dark seemed to quicken in tandem with his own heartbeat. *Well at least I must be alive*, he thought. The recognition of this fact sharpened his awareness, causing the calm darkness to pulse faster, beginning to move and shift, as if in recognition of his consciousness. *Sleep*, he thought, *get back to sleep, away from all thoughts of where and how, sleeping like a baby.*

But where was Mum? He couldn't sleep like a baby without her. Suddenly his memory began to return, images of terror shattering the calm darkness pulling him up, twisting and screaming to the brutal light of reality, pain searing his skin, the wounds that lay raw on his face and chest fizzing into life.

And what a twisted reality he faced. Eyelids fused open, he found himself bound tightly to some kind of wooden structure, arms spread out like a crucifix. The smell of damp and decay assaulted him, punishing his nostrils and causing him to inhale in shallow gasping breaths. It was still dark, but not dark enough to hide the twisting shapes of the Nasties that crawled over and around each other like bees in a hive. He was in the nest, trapped like a fly in a spider's web.

Aunt Val deliberated for exactly twenty minutes before she called the police. She didn't want to get Mathilda in trouble but she couldn't just let her go off with those people. Cathy seemed nice, but the man—well, he looked crazy. It took a while to get through to someone but based on what she had heard on the news that was no surprise. Therwick was a big story and the police were at full stretch. Eventually she was transferred to a weary sounding policeman called Duckworth. At least he was a local, she thought as she recognized his soft accent. That was better than one of those city policemen she had seen on the TV. They wouldn't listen to her concerns.

PC Carl Duckworth's head was pounding. He had only seen photos of the scout camp, but his partner had actually been there and smelled the coppery blood that was splattered all over the place, seen what remained of the torn bodies of the children and their parents. Only old Archibald remained. All the local police knew he had nothing to do with this carnage, despite the declarations from the cold-eyed CID officer that they had a prime suspect. Carl had seen poor Archibald through the hatch in the cell door, sobbing like a child and begging for the light to be left on. He didn't look like a killer. He just looked like he had lost his mind, whimpering about creatures that fell from the trees. Demons, he called them.

Carl grimaced. There was something or someone out there in the woods, but not demons. They would catch this madman and he would wish he was in the circles of hell by the time they had finished with him. The city boys had quickly and efficiently isolated all of the local police, relegating them to manning the phones and dealing with the numerous requests from the press and calls from local people. They were just local plod now, apparently no use to the investigation despite all their local knowledge. Though quietly furious they had little choice but to comply. Like a glorified call centre, Carl thought as he snatched up the ringing phone on his desk.

'Valerie Crook,' he repeated. It was a name he remembered, kind of stood out in his line of work. Miss Crook. He remembered she was a Miss. She had been at great pains to spell that out when he had been sitting in her painfully tidy and ordered front room, what three years ago, with the little girl, Mathilda.

You don't forget those type of experiences, he reflected, not when you have kids of your own. And you couldn't blame Miss Crook for her bewildered and slightly horrified reaction as the enormity of the tragedy sank in. Lots of lives had been turned inside out that day. And now she was on the phone, put through to him as another local crank, but from what he could understand, the CID staff must have misread this one. Mathilda had gone missing, heading off with two strangers—or at least nearly strangers, she said she recognized the woman from around town—to investigate the woods around Therwick. Miss Crook was particularly concerned about the man she went with, whom she pointedly described as 'a bit deranged.'

He was bored and frustrated, tied to his desk while all around him his beloved town was in chaos. If CID had allowed this one to pass through to him, he was well within his rights to follow it up, wasn't he?

Maybe he could take a drive out to the woods, that's where the action was. Miss Crook had said they planned to get there by heading in from the timber roads on the outskirts of town, she had heard that much. Couldn't hurt, could it? He felt slightly protective towards the girl, she probably needed a bit of guidance. After all she had been through, it wouldn't be a surprise if she was getting up to a bit of mischief or even if she had just found herself in with the wrong crowd. *Better check it out,* he thought as he headed out the back of the police station to where the squad car was parked.

Chapter 23

They must look quite a sight, Cathy thought. Bash led the way, his axe in hand, closely followed by Mathilda who held her bow across her with an arrow poised and ready. It was just as well they hadn't bumped into anyone. The woods were normally popular with dog walkers and mountain bikes, but they were conspicuously absent today. The police would have stopped most of them, but she thought the strangely poisonous atmosphere may have meant a few would have turned back anyway. The woods really didn't feel right at all. The sun was dipping in and out as the tree line got progressively higher around them. This part of Therwick woods was still relatively untouched and Cathy could almost imagine how they might have been in times past when they were truly wild. She couldn't shake the feeling they were somehow disconnecting from reality with each step. Up ahead Bash continued to monitor his axe, its glow acting like a magical compass. The going was tougher now they had left the logging track and she prayed they would find Charlie before it started to get dark. The thought of Charlie being out there somewhere, on his own, possibly hurt, was unbearable. She prayed that Alex's talisman, the amulet, was keeping him safe from harm.

For her part Mathilda was caught between manic excitement and pounding fear. Her skin felt like it was crackling with electricity, the bow a live thing in her hands, an extension of her. She wanted to fight. She knew it was serious, but God it was like being in a real life film. Forget music, boys or any other stuff that got her group of friends excited, this was where it was at. It was all she could do not to grin.

Bash was less enthusiastic, his mind a muddle of worries and fear. He had been in this situation before and the memories of Italy and the raw terror of fighting for his life were fresh. He realised now he had been an easy tragedy for Alex to exploit. Too drunk to really care what he was doing, he had been reckless and half mad. The drinking and the hunting had been a toxic mix, each fuelling the other. Only now did he question what type of friend Alex had been. Being a Watcher, supposedly one of the good guys, hadn't meant Alex was necessarily a good man or a good husband and father. But Bash was different now. He had Cathy and Mathilda to think about as well as Charlie. A ten-year-old entrusted with all their safety. It was like a bad joke. He was determined to make it right. This time would pay for all his foul-ups. He gripped his axe tighter still. The blade glowed a dazzling blue, the edges of flame spilling down it and covering his hands in a shimmering coat. He would make it right.

Beleth watched the boy closely as he struggled against the bindings that held him tightly to the broken rafters of the building. They all struggled, humans and Watchers alike. Beleth had seen them doing so for millennia.

The toxicity of humanity had undone the Watchers. They were a spent force in the universe, with only this child left to fulfil the purpose for which they had been created. The boy's father had been the one they wanted. He hadn't known the other Watchers had deserted him, some of them succumbing to the temptation of power, riches and blessed normality that Beleth had so carefully offered them. The ones that didn't had been killed. It didn't matter, either way was good enough. The Watchers had become magicians in a time when no-one believed in magic, so they had all fallen at his feet, one way or another.

Except the boy's father. He had been different. He had enjoyed the hunt so very much, only realising too late that he had overestimated his powers and the reliability of his fellow Watchers, his precious family. It was a pity he'd had the foresight to give the child his amulet. That had made dispatching the father easier, although the wounds Beleth took in that final battle had pushed it to the limit, forcing it to lose itself in the inter world for years to heal and recover.

But now the protection the amulet offered made killing the boy more difficult than it would have otherwise been. He would die, of course, but maddeningly not without some sacrifice.

Around Beleth the Nasties writhed, impatient for the kill and the feast that would follow. It flexed its massive talons, itching to run them through the flickering flames that still encased the boy, preventing the killing blow. It was the amulet that allowed this, a last line of defence when the body was weak and injured.

The boy was powerful, that much was clear, but he was just a boy. He wasn't yet fully equipped to fight. If they could remove the amulet he would be exposed and then he would be taken. But how? Beleth mused. Only a Watcher could remove the amulet and only of their own accord. That was why the battle had always been eternal. Beleth had the other four amulets, stored between the worlds where they would never be found. Either handed to it in return for empty promises and the petty power and riches humans craved, or ripped from dying fingers, the result was the same. What would encourage a boy to give up something so precious? What did a boy value beyond all else?

Cathy saw it first. The old house was a part of Therwick mythology. As children they had scared themselves half to death with stories of the murders that were meant to have happened there. She had forgotten it even existed until now. The crumbling walls that formed the boundary of the estate were the first sign of civilization since leaving the track an hour or two ago. In places the walls had collapsed entirely and been consumed by the forest floor, but by following its broken line they found themselves gathered at the main gate, its metal frame encased in ivy. The sun had gone in, and beneath the dense trees the day had switched to twilight. They huddled together in the shadow of the gate, faces cast blue with the vibrant glow from Bash's axe. They spoke in whispers.

'What now then?' asked Cathy. 'Is he here? I think he is you know, I can feel it.' The horror of losing Charlie crashed in on Cathy, causing her to catch her breath. 'Please—can we just do something?'

'The house. He must be in there, where else could he be?' replied Mathilda as she stared down the overgrown driveway that wound its way to the main house. 'Look at it —it's horrible.' Bash looked up at the treetops, which had started to rustle secretively. He turned to Cathy.

'Please, Cath—stay here, you won't be able to help in there and if we don't come out or one of us gets hurt we will need you. You heard what they did at that scout camp, they'll kill you in a heartbeat. Leave this to us, I can get him back but not if I need to be looking out for you as well.'

Mathilda thought she saw something. A flicker of movement through the trees that shrouded the house from view. She brought her bow up in a smooth movement and tracked the arrow left to right, the tip dripping blue fire that spluttered and fizzed as it hit the floor. *Maybe I'm imagining things*, she thought, her heart racing.

In the cellar of the house Beleth raised its massive head, its eyes blinking in slow unison. They were here, and so was the mother. It almost chuckled, it was perfect, it thought. The Nasties around it circled up into the air, hungrily awaiting its order. The nearest turned on each other in a flurry of claws and teeth, splattering thick black blood onto those below. *Bring her to me*, it commanded.

'Bash, I'm coming with you, there's no way I'm standing out here while you two go in there playing superheroes. He's my son.' They stared at each other, neither wanting to back down. 'But, Cathy,' he started, before all hell broke loose.

They came from nowhere, materialising out of thin air around her. A swarm of claws grabbed her and pulled her up into the treetops. Neither Bash nor Mathilda had time to react. No sooner had they arrived than they were gone. Her screams were cut short as the Nasties wrenched her out of this world, through a whirling black maelstrom of nothingness, before depositing her with a crash onto the floor of the cellar.

She pushed herself up with her hands, her hair hanging over her face. The smell of rot and death that surrounded her was indescribable. Looking up she saw Charlie tethered to the wall, his head hanging limply, the stuttering flames around him casting a faint light around the cellar. Seeing him spiked her into action, and ignoring the foul muck that caked the floor she pulled herself to her feet and started towards him. Around her the Nasties moved steadily back with each step she took, a wall of creatures that she couldn't see, although somewhere inside her she knew they must be there.

Beleth watched with interest. It held back the horde which crowded the woman, inches away and so eager to strike. The others needed dealing with, they would try to rescue the boy and it didn't want to be distracted. At its command, half of the horde peeled away from the woman and spiralled away from the cellar, screaming delight at the chance to kill and feed. The remaining fell back as Beleth moved carefully across the cellar, back bent low where the ceiling remained. Time to reveal itself, it thought with something akin to amusement.

Chapter 24

Outside Bash and Mathilda were approaching the main entrance of the house, running as quickly as they could through the thick vegetation. The door hung ajar, like a slack mouth, as they raced up the steps to the entrance. Bash's axe was dazzlingly bright. Mathilda avoided looking at it as they peered into the gloom, her eyes slowly adjusting to the darkness within.

'Which way?' she asked. The interior was strewn with debris from where the roof had partially collapsed. Pools of fetid water gathered just inside the doorway. A grand staircase ran up the centre of the entrance hall. Either side of the stairs, two hallways led to the rear of the house and into darkness.

'That way,' said Bash. 'To the back of the house, they will be somewhere dark, a cellar or something.'

Mathilda didn't even see the first of the Nasties that appeared. She unleashed her arrow on instinct. It cut a flaming path through the gloom, spearing the writhing creature to the wall. She stared at it, wide-eyed.

'No time to admire your shot,' said Bash, nodding his head in the direction of the main hall. Mathilda followed his gaze. The Nasties were pouring down the staircase. A torrent of teeth and claws.

Tears ran down Cathy's face, cutting twin paths through the mud and filth caked across it. Her son, her Charlie, hung limply from the ceiling. The flames that had burned so strongly around him now flickered and stuttered. Beneath them she could see the cuts and lacerations the Nasties had made to his flesh. He had held them at bay, but was now exhausted. With all her strength she dragged a broken chest of drawers that had been left to rot in the corner of the cellar over to where Charlie hung. The wood was soft and spongy but she thought it should take her weight. Beyond the darkness she could feel the presence of the Nasties. They had to be here, but for whatever reason they were holding back. Her flesh crawled at the thought of them, unseen, gathering around her, but Charlie needed her and that thought smothered all else. She clambered up onto the drawers, her foot crunching softly through the rotting wood, although it held her for now.

He must have sensed her presence as his head raised slowly, although oddly his eyes remained shut and his mouth was slack as if he was in a deep sleep. Puzzled, she reached for him, her eyes searching along his arms for the knots that held him fastened to the old timber rafters. To her horror a huge taloned hand materialized. It gripped Charlie's hair and now she understood it was this that was holding his head up. The form lengthened, flowing into a muscled arm as thick as a tree trunk, and up to a shoulder and suddenly the vast head and neck of Beleth. Cathy screamed in terror as Beleth smiled, staring at her with a myriad red eyes. 'Welcome,' it rasped.

They came like fury. Pouring down on Bash and Mathilda from the staircase, squeezing up through the gaps in the floor, with yet more appearing from nowhere, popping into existence in the air around them. Bash pulled her towards him.

'Stay close,' he shouted. 'Pick your shots.' She nodded, pulling back the bow and firing another arrow into the head of a foul looking creature that had rushed forward from the pack. Her hand reached back over her shoulder and seamlessly strung another arrow from the flaming quiver on her back. 'How many do you have?' asked Bash.

'About twenty, I think,' Mathilda replied.

'Use them wisely and recover them so you can fire again,' he said. 'Stay close.'

Bash tightened his grip on the axe with both hands, took in a deep breath and set to work, the flaming blade quickly a blur of movement as he cut and hacked his way into the Nasties that leapt at them.

Carl pulled the 4x4 jeep up next to the small red car. He had taken the only one they had, swiping the keys from the desk sergeant before he had time to object. The car fitted the description Valerie Crook had provided. He touched the bonnet. It was cold. They had obviously left it a while ago. It had taken him longer than expected to find them. There were a lot more ways into Therwick woods than he had remembered. After a number of blind alleys he had at last found a clue as to their whereabouts. From here there was only one way they could have gone. Down into the woods. He was no tracker but even he could see the scuffed footprints that led that way were made recently. The 4x4 would help him make up some time. He had been on his advanced off-road course and knew he could drive it almost anywhere.

Putting it in gear, he revved the engine loudly and skidded off down the narrowing track that he knew led to the old house. It was not far from where they had found poor Simon's dead pony. He gritted his teeth as his stomach rolled uncomfortably. Something wasn't right. He had a sense of strands pulling together but he couldn't yet see the picture they were forming. He looked at the shotgun that was secured to the dashboard; the lock that held it within its fitting was shiny and new. He had never had cause to release the gun before. In fact in the whole time he had been a policeman he had only heard of one of his colleagues using one. It was for emergencies only and there was hell to pay, not to mention a stack of paperwork to complete, if it was released without good reason. He hoped his standard issue Taser and baton would be sufficient. He was sure they would, but he was glad the shotgun was there all the same.

The woman had fainted. A shame but perhaps her collapsed form would have the desired effect on the boy when Beleth decided to wake him again. It sniffed hungrily at the air. The Nasties edged closer, sensing its excitement. The amulet still provided a thin layer of flame. It would hurt, even though the boy was weak, slowly searing his thick skin and the tender flesh beneath. But it would be worth it. The boy would see his mother, see her helplessness and he would do as Beleth asked.

Beleth grimaced, the flames around the boy pulsing brighter and more hungrily as it pushed its huge hand through them. Pain, such a human sensation, ignited in it. 'Wake,' it hissed. 'See what I have, Watcher, see your precious mother so close to death.'

The whirling flames around Charlie inched greedily up Beleth's arm, the flesh beneath bubbling and beginning to char. 'Wake,' it insisted, its talon pushing through the boy's shoulder, piercing the skin and scraping the bone beneath. The pain, so intense, snapped his eyes open, wide and shocked, as he screamed himself fully awake. Focus returned and Charlie looked into the eyes of Beleth. The beast had withdrawn its talon from his shoulder. It held its burnt arm aloft, thin wisps of smoke rising from the cracked skin. The Nasties curled and spiralled around it, licking the wounds, mewling and hissing like cats.

'My children care for me,' it mused. 'Family is so very important, don't you think?' It chuckled, a horrible throaty burble that bounced around the walls, sending the Nasties wild with delight. The monster's words drilled into Charlie's mind, imprinted rather than heard. How could it speak, he thought, was it speaking or was it all in his mind? What was happening? He had been in and out of consciousness and felt adrift.

All thoughts suddenly stopped. The Beleth held his mum aloft, its claws gripping her thick hair, pulling it taut against her scalp, her body hanging a few feet above the cellar floor.

'It's over, Watcher. You are finished. Your friends are dead and your mother will follow. Unless...'

Charlie stared at his mum. Was she alive? He thought so. Her chest was rising and falling. He stared back into the eyes of the beast, fear and anger competing in his chest.

'Unless you want me to spare her. Yes ....I could do that for you, but only if you give me your amulet. Take it off and I will let your mother live.' Its eyes narrowed into cat-like slits.

'You don't want this life you have inherited, child. Watching is thankless, you could ask your brothers, if any were alive to listen.' Beleth grinned. 'I will do you this small act of mercy, remove the amulet and I will release you from your duties. This way will spare both you and her any more suffering.'

Charlie found his hands untied. His hands moved without him thinking to his neck, his fingers seeking out the chain and stone that hung beneath it. Its voice was so horribly convincing. The chain solidified in his fingers. Beleth leaned forward in anticipation. It would be swift. As soon as the chain was gone he would rip open the boy's throat and the Watchers would be no more. The one that remained under his control would be killed and the Nasties would rise. It had been thousands of years since they had been this close to victory. The horde howled with delight.

Chapter 25

In the main hall Bash and Mathilda fought on.

The floor was littered with the fading corpses of Nasties that had been cut or speared by their efforts. Bash was near exhaustion. His shoulders and arms screamed for mercy as he swung his axe again at one that scuttled along the wall, before launching itself at them. Mathilda backed into a doorway at the end of the left-hand corridor from the entrance hall. A staircase led down to darkness. A cellar. Where else.

She checked her quiver. Four arrows remained, as well as the one she had strung in her bow. She had used the others multiple times but found the flame faded after the second or third kill. After that point they were useless. Bash's axe, on the other hand, just seemed to keep on going. It was just as well. If she had killed thirty of them, he must have killed double that amount. Thick blood and gore were splattered all over his face and body. He reminded her of those Roman soldiers they had studied in history at school. They had battled for days until they almost fought whilst asleep, killing by instinct. Mathilda knew that time was running out. They had to find Cathy and Charlie. Only with Charlie at their side could they really defeat the Nasties. At some point the axe and her arrows would fade. The magic would leave and then they would die.

Bash flung a dying Nastie to the floor. He could see Mathilda beckoning him over to the darkened doorway. The Nasties that remained were keeping their distance. There couldn't be more than ten of them left up here, although they were some of the larger ones. No two looked exactly alike, but they all resembled some kind of freakish animal. They all had teeth and claws. They circled Bash, measuring the distance between him and Mathilda.

He was amazed at her composure. She had fought well, calm when the horde had first attacked, her aim perfect. She had made the most of her arrows, wrenching them from the quivering bodies of dying Nasties, but the fading magic in her weapon had unsettled her. He could see fear creeping into her eyes. He felt it too. His right arm was numb from a crippling blow delivered by a powerful Nastie. Beneath the thick black blood that caked him, his own blood flowed. With each minute he felt weaker and without a Watcher, without Charlie, he knew they couldn't survive another full-on attack. They had killed a lot of them, but there would be many more. Bash was sure of it. Swinging his axe in front of him like a flame to ward off a pack of wolves, he moved down the hallway to where Mathilda stood. The Nasties hissed and spat, popping in and out of existence, edging closer but for now unwilling to attack.

In the cellar Beleth saw they were coming. It could see them through the eyes of its brothers up in the house. A flicker of tension passed across its snarling face. Let them come, it thought, it would be too late by then.

The amulet resisted. Charlie's fingers pulled the chain, now fully materialized from under his skin, but the amulet itself held fast. When he pulled harder it rose up, its bright blue light tinted red as it puckered up under the skin of his neck, but it refused to release itself. Beleth lifted his mum closer to Charlie's face and gently ran its huge claw along the line of her throat. A thin line of blood began to flow from her neck and her eyelids fluttered as she awoke from her faint. 'Mum!' he screamed. 'No—don't hurt her.'

He pulled harder still and finally the amulet relented, coming out from under his skin. The stone flashed a brief and brilliant blue before fading slowly to grey, like an ember pulled from a fire. Charlie felt the power drain from him. It was a curious feeling, like a switch had been turned off, leaving him slightly breathless and dizzy. The flames that surrounded him flickered on and off. He realised he needed to concentrate, to consciously focus, to keep the flames around him alive. His fuel supply was gone—he was running on empty.

'Now let her go. I've done as you asked,' he pleaded.

'But of course,' the Beleth snarled. With a flick of its arm it threw Cathy across the cellar. She hit the wall with a sickening crunch. Before Charlie had time to react the Nasties seized him. The amulet dangled from the chain gripped in his tightly clenched hand. In panic he tried to call forth the flame, but the feeling of energy and power refused to obey his will, dancing out of his reach.

'It's over,' Beleth whispered triumphantly, raising its claws above its head to strike the killing blow.

Bash and Mathilda stumbled down the staircase to the cellar. Behind them the Nasties that followed screeched and clawed, the screams bouncing off the walls and making their heads spin. Bash looked in alarm at his axe. The fire was fading. Mathilda ran ahead. She couldn't raise her bow in the cramped staircase and she prayed Bash was looking out for her. Ahead was a door. She couldn't see if it was locked, but from behind it she heard a triumphant roar. Without thinking she launched herself at it, hitting it hard with her shoulder. The door was rotten and tore away from its hinges. She hit the floor on the other side, rolling over and to her feet, pulling back her bowstring in a fluid motion. The arrow, clinging on to the last of it flame, flew straight and true, punching through the swiping claw of Beleth, causing it to miss Charlie's face by inches. It fell to the floor as the Nasties rushed to their stricken master. The amulet slipped from its hand, dropping to the cellar floor, lost amongst the muck and filth.

The Nasties in the cellar turned as one towards the two intruders. Bash reached Mathilda, turning back towards the staircase in case the ones from upstairs tried to attack. Mathilda strung another arrow, cursing the stuttering flame. 'Charlie,' she screamed. 'Help us.'

Beleth howled, the flame from the arrow spreading up its arm. The moment was lost. The killing blow so long awaited was denied. Its anger knew no limits.

'Kill them all,' it screamed. The horde leaped forward. Bash could only look as they rushed towards them. His axe was dead in his hands, the flame extinguished. Mathilda's arrow gave up its flame, the blue residue scattering into the air. They were defenceless.

Charlie saw the horde of Nasties charge at Bash and Mathilda. To his right he saw the stricken figure of his mum. She was alive, groggily trying to pick herself up from the floor.

'Charlie,' she croaked, the call catching the attention of the Nasties, some of which then peeled off in her direction. Bash and Mathilda saw what was happening and ran over to her, brandishing their now useless weapons. Charlie looked desperately for the fallen amulet, his hands sweeping through the sticky filth of the cellar floor. They was going to die if he couldn't find it. He whimpered, feeling every inch a ten-year-old boy. What had they been thinking?

Chapter 26

The 4x4 bounced and jolted though the trees. The track had long since departed, and it was all Carl could do to hang on to the steering wheel as the car pitched this way and that. The old house should be up ahead and if he had his bearings right, he should find the access track again, which would be a relief after the battering the car had taken. The house was the stuff of legend amongst the older Therwick policemen. The last time the media had been interested in Therwick was when the scandal at the house had become national news. Devil worship and murder had a tendency to attract a bit of interest. The more lurid headlines had been cut out of the papers of the time and frozen in a picture frame that hung in the canteen back at the station.

Through the bug-splattered windscreen, the trees began to thin and to his left Carl could see the cracked remnants of the road leading to the house. As he hauled the steering wheel to his right, the car bumped up and onto the comparatively even surface and Carl accelerated towards the house. It revealed itself in flashes through the trees as if it was playing hide and seek. Again a feeling of helpless inevitability washed over him, as though he was stuck on a rollercoaster and had to just hang in there until the ride was over.

When they had looked for Simon, the forensics team had picked over the house from top to bottom like white-suited maggots on a corpse. They had found nothing, leaving only with a vague sense of disquiet, like they had been tricked somehow. For whatever reason, call it a premonition or just a policeman's instinct, he knew in his gut that he was going to find something at the house.

That feeling didn't ease when he turned off the car's ignition and stepped out onto the driveway in front of the main entrance.

Beyond the soft crunch of gravel under his feet there was another noise. A sound beneath the everyday, like he was hearing it from underneath water. Carl peered through the broken door, flicking on his torch and playing the beam across the hallway and up against the wall behind the staircase. He blinked. His eyes were seeing something but it was like a transfer overlaying reality, flickering in and out. One minute the broken hallway, the next dark shapes scattered across the floor. The feeling of doubling left him feeling dizzy and sick.

Without hesitating he went back to the car and carefully unlocked the housing that held the shotgun. *Paperwork be damned,* he thought, he just wanted the solid sense of security that washed over him when he pushed the stock of the gun into his shoulder.

He switched on his torch again and moved carefully into the house, the beam of light tracking the barrel of his gun as he headed towards the foot of the staircase. A muffled noise came to him again, like a scream, and he turned in response, heading to his right towards another staircase that led down into darkness. It occurred to him that despite all his training he hadn't called in his whereabouts to the station. Peering into the black below him, he regretted this uncharacteristic lapse of procedure.

Every inch of him yelled *turn back,* but a sound of screaming was building in his head. Not heard in his ears, but pulsing directly into his brain. Procedure be damned, he thought, raising the shotgun to eye level and running faster down the crumbling stairs to the cellar.

The Nasties slowed, circling Cathy, Bash and Mathilda, enclosing them, enjoying their fear, tasting it in the air, saliva flowing like rivers from lines of razor sharp teeth. Beleth pushed its way through them, struggling to control their appetites, wanting the satisfaction of the kill itself. The arrow in its hand burned and with a snarl of rage it clenched its fist, shattering it, the burning fragments falling to the floor at its feet. The boy was looking for the amulet, snivelling like the lost child he was. Beleth wanted revenge, to tear and slash. The boy would wait a moment. It wanted him to see his friends die first, screaming and begging for mercy.

Carl jumped down the last three steps, landing squarely, the gun and flashlight sweeping the room. *What the hell,* he thought? To his right he could see the girl, Mathilda, standing with a man and a woman. Over the far side of the cellar, a boy was on his hands and knees furiously searching for something, their pale faces reflected in the torchlight. God, did that man have an axe in his hands? He swept the shotgun round, levelling it on the man next to Mathilda.

'Put the weapon down, sir,' he shouted. 'Now.' His finger tightened on the trigger.

'Help us!' Mathilda screamed.

Carl was confused—help them? With what? He blinked and again there was that unsettling doubling sensation. What the hell was going on? he thought. There was something there. His eyes tried to focus and for a brief second he saw a flurry of movement, a flash of claws and numerous red eyes, before maddeningly the images disappeared in a haze of static. The boy continued to search through the debris on the floor. Carl moved closer to Mathilda, his gun pointed at the man who held the axe. Their attention had returned to the centre of the cellar, where they stared seemingly into nothingness.

'I repeat, put down the weapon and step away from the girl,' he said.

Why were they ignoring him—what were they looking at? He rubbed his hand over his face. His eyes ached. Suddenly they moved back towards him, the woman screamed and the man pushed both her and Mathilda behind him, brandishing his axe at thin air. He found himself next to Mathilda who he saw, to his amazement, was pointing a bow and arrow at the same empty space that seemed to fascinate the man. The woman grabbed him by the shoulder and pointed in front of them. 'It's coming,' she said, shuddering, her nails digging into his arm. The static that cracked and distorted his sight cleared and finally Carl saw what was happening. The Nasties parted and from between them Beleth lurched forward. He shouted in terror, bringing the shotgun up to his shoulder and firing directly at the massive head that loomed out of the darkness.

The sound of the gunshot echoed around the cellar. Everything seemed to stop for a moment. Carl stared in shock through the wisps of smoke that drifted up from the gun barrel, its sharp smell like fireworks and burning leaves. Around him he could see the writhing shapes of the Nasties and directly ahead a sense of total darkness where the massive creature had been. The three of them drew together, collectively holding their breath. In the darkness eyes opened, red and cruel. One after another they appeared, swiftly followed by a huge crescent mouth lined with needle-sharp teeth. Carl pulled Cathy behind him, raising the shotgun again.

'Don't waste your time, my friend,' the dark skinned man said sadly, looking steadily at him. 'Bullets won't stop it—nothing can stop it now.'

Charlie heard the gunshot and in the flash of light that accompanied it he saw a man in a policeman's uniform standing next to his mum. Hope danced in his chest; help had arrived. Perhaps they would be safe, he thought, before any notion was crushed by the slowly rising shape of Beleth, its massive presence moving through the Nasties towards his mum and his friends.

Bash stepped forward, his axe held aloft. To his side the policeman was frozen in shock, staring incredulously at the looming shape of the monster. He couldn't blame him, it was not exactly your average day at the office. Sadly the game seemed to be up. He knew he didn't want to go down without a fight. He would do his best to protect Charlie and Cathy as he had promised, then he could at least die with some dignity. It beat being the town drunk anyway. For the first time in years he didn't feel like a drink would help. He almost chuckled at the irony. Gritting his teeth, he started to spin his axe, faster and faster. *This time pays for all*, he thought before launching himself at Beleth.

Charlie saw Bash swipe a glancing blow across Beleth's face. It snarled displeasure before plunging its claws into and then through his chest. It raised Bash above its head, its face splitting into a toxic grin of delight. The axe fell from his hand and he twitched like a fish caught on a spear, his blood pouring down Beleth's arms and splattering onto its upturned face. Mathilda screamed, unleashing an arrow that uncharacteristically missed the target, thudding into the wall just to the left of its huge head.

Beleth lowered its arms. Bash's broken body slid off its claws and fell to the ground. Cathy scrambled forward cradling him, her hands desperately trying to stem the flow of blood from multiple wounds. Mathilda strung one of her few remaining arrows, pulling back the bow and aiming it at Beleth, tears streaming down her face. It turned towards them, its huge tongue slavering around its face, scooping up the splashes of blood and pulling them down into its throat. It gasped, relishing the sour taste. The girl's useless bow wavered, betraying her shaking hands. She would taste all the sweeter for her fear, it thought.

Charlie could see Beleth lining up its next killing blow. Around it the Nasties capered and screamed with excitement. Smaller ones darted forward to lap Bash's blood from the floor, whilst others reached out to claw and scratch his mum and Mathilda. The ten-year-old boy in him wanted to curl up and weep, to hide. But the part of him that was a Watcher resisted. All of a sudden it felt like he walked with a twin version of himself, older, wiser and more confident. Ready to step into his skin and take control. The ten-year-old Charlie Picker embraced that version of himself, becoming one with it, praying it would last. A feeling of controlled anger flowed over him, suddenly igniting flames that danced over his skin and burned behind his eyes. In response the amulet flickered into life on the floor just to his left. It had been there all along. He snatched it up, holding it tightly in his fist, but he didn't feel like he needed it. He was the last of the Watchers and he felt ready to

142

fight. He pulled himself to his feet, the flames rising higher and brighter around him, burning off the muck and filth that caked his skin. Around him spheres of bright blue flame formed, spiralling lazily, one, then four, then eight, then twelve. Faster and faster they turned until they crisscrossed in a blaze of blue fire. He needed to finish what his father had started. The flames started to gather, a whirlwind of blue bursting from his feet to the ceiling of the cellar where they pooled as a broiling lake of flame. With a cry Charlie pushed the torrent of flame from his hands, directing it like a hose at the Nasties that scampered around behind Beleth. They burned and screamed.

At the same time Bash's axe flickered like a defective bulb, strobing faster and faster before bursting into flame on the floor. The arrow strung in Mathilda's bow did not even hesitate. It roared into life, the flame stronger than ever before. Mathilda poked Carl with the tip of her bow.

'Do you see that axe?' she said. 'Take it, take it and help me.'

Beleth turned and looked at the boy in disbelief, the savage joy of killing the man fading at what it saw. How was he doing it? He was meant to be powerless but instead he burned brighter than ever before. Enough was enough. It wouldn't be bested by a boy, by a child. They would all feel the true power of Beleth, the Infinite One.

Mathilda schooled Carl in the arts of Nastie killing, using her bow to pick off targets, then darting forward to retrieve the flaming arrows as one after another was impaled. Carl stumbled along at her side, swiping the axe at anything that came near him. In a frenzy of rage Beleth turned and headed towards where Charlie was standing. Shaking its head from side to side, like an enraged bull readying itself for one last charge at a matador, it gathered speed, racing across the floor, before leaping into the air, its body elongating into a spear of claws and teeth. Instinctively he created a shield of flame around himself, setting himself firmly within it, braced for the impact. Beleth crashed into him, rolling over the top of the shield, the flames scorching its body, but landing cat-like on all fours. Within his sanctuary- Charlie shuddered. It was so strong. With a force of will, he pushed the shield away from himself, fashioning it into a disc of flame that he then threw with all his strength at the crouching shape of Beleth. It sliced through the air, whirring past its shoulder, cutting deep into its flesh before breaking up as it smashed into the wall. The floor above shook with the impact, old plaster and wood raining down into the cellar. Before Beleth had time to retaliate he sent a stream of flame from his hands, pouring out everything he could. The flames engulfed Beleth who inched towards Charlie like a man walking in a high wind, stooped forward as its flesh was flayed from its body into a stream of foul dust behind it. Its face was fixed in a grimace of hatred. With increasing alarm Charlie realized he couldn't hold it back, its progress was relentless.

Throughout Mathilda had been casting anxious glances over to the battle between Charlie and Beleth. The Nasties that remained had retreated to the middle of the cellar. Mathilda had four arrows left, and there was only one that she couldn't retrieve. It was stuck in the cellar ceiling where it fizzed and spat sparks of blue. They had reached a stalemate, eying each other but unwilling to attack. Carl, who under the circumstances had performed admirably, was helping Cathy attend to Bash. He was alive but only just. They needed to get him help soon. With alarm she saw Beleth edging closer to Charlie, the two of them locked in battle.

Beleth was within a few feet of Charlie now, the flames roaring around them both. Charlie looked in desperation at its myriad eyes. Mathilda drew back her bow, taking careful aim at one of those burning red points in the darkness.

It grinned, despite the huge damage it was taking, reaching forward with a huge claw, grabbing Charlie by the shoulder.

'Shall we?' it rasped, before he was whirled away into the inky nothingness of the inter world. In the same moment the arrow was released, streaking across the cellar, punching into the wall. They had vanished.

Chapter 27

The place Charlie found himself in reminded him of a hall of mirrors. He had been in one at a fair with his friends a few years ago, when the green at the edge of Therwick played host to it at the end of the summer. That had been fun, at least to start with, as they had run around the dizzying maze, disoriented and laughing. But the feeling of distortion had become overwhelming and they had been relieved to stumble out of the exit into the fading summer evening light. He felt like that now in this strange inter world. The reality from which he had been snatched could be seen in flashes, like reflections, but shaded and distant, blooming suddenly out of the darkness before disappearing just as quickly. It was in this hall of mirrors that the Beleth stalked him. Its voice was sometimes close, and then far away, toying with him.

'Nowhere to run, child,' it hissed. 'It's forever in here, between the worlds.'

Charlie almost heard a sigh in its voice, as if it regretted the things it had to say.

'Your father is in here somewhere. At least what remains of him. He came here, foolishly thinking he could survive in my world. He screamed a great deal before he died.' It paused. 'When I am done with you, I will return for your mother and your friends. They will all die, but you know this, don't you? You know that you cannot save them.'

Charlie spun round this way and that. Shimmering shapes danced away at the edges of his vision. 'Where are you?' he cried. 'Show yourself.'

The flames around him rippled with his growing anger. Beleth appeared ahead of him, lurching suddenly out of the gloom. An instinctive burst of flame from his hands raced towards it but passed straight through the image, fading to nothing in the endless distance. Beleth's throaty laughter bubbled around him, echoing madly in his ears. Charlie stared to run.

Back in the cellar the last of the Nasties were on the move. Only nine remained of the vast horde created by Beleth. Some of them had started to clamber up the broken walls and through the gaps in the ceiling. For whatever reason it seemed they could no longer zip in and out of the world like they had before. That magic seemed to have disappeared with their king. It made them easier to keep an eye on and that was a relief whilst Carl struggled to carry Bash up the staircase. They had all agreed they couldn't wait any longer to get him to a hospital. It was only as Carl moved carefully up the staircase that Mathilda noticed his hair had turned completely white. It had been that type of day.

Charlie had been gone for about ten minutes and it was taking all of Cathy's strength not to go completely crazy. She had lost so much to this madness, first her husband and now her son. She held Bash's axe tightly in her hand, its glow reassuring her that he must still be OK, wherever he was, but her hands trembled, each shudder a measure of her desperation.

In the inter world Charlie continued to run.

It was like being in a terrible dream; no matter how fast or in what direction he thought he travelled, the looming presence and manic laughter of Beleth remained constant. At some point the amulet had slipped out of his hand. He barely registered it, panic threatening to overwhelm him. Occasionally glimpses of reality appeared through gossamer-thin patches in the walls around him, but no sooner had he seen them than they faded away like smoke.

He looked over his shoulder, sure he would see Beleth creeping nimbly behind him, but instead he saw only nothingness, save for a pinprick of brilliant blue light that could only be his lost amulet. It was too late to turn back and retrieve it, and in fact even as he looked it was becoming harder to see where back actually was. The grey walls between here and reality bruised with occasional movement and Charlie could sense there were still further worlds beyond them, populated by God knows what. Huge shadows passed along the walls, shapes like nothing his imagination could contemplate, creatures beyond his conception pushing against the thin layers that separated the worlds. He could sense hunger and a crackling madness that was overwhelming. He felt so small, such a tiny cog in the endless wheel of the multiverse. How would he ever be able to protect himself from Beleth, never mind all from all the strange and terrible forces that moved behind the grey spaces of the inter world?

His courage wavered. He wanted to rest, to curl up on a sofa next to his mum like he used to. It was only a matter of months ago when he would have been doing just that, safe in his little house, not lost in a strange world. He was quite big for his age, but he didn't feel big now, he felt scared and he wanted to go home.

Without warning, Beleth materialized from the gloom and hit Charlie with a sickening crunch, its claws driving through the flames and pinning him to the floor. His breath was forced out of him and unable to even scream he stared up into its slavering jaws. Strands of saliva spiralled down, fizzing and popping as they reached the thin layer of flame that encased him.

'I am even stronger in here, boy,' it growled. 'And I see you dropped your precious amulet. Losing it twice in one day, your father would not have been impressed—no, not impressed at all.'

Charlie struggled, the pain incredible, but its claws held him fast. 'I grow weary of all this running,' it said, digging its claws deeper still into him before twisting them slowly. 'I think it is time for you and me to say farewell.'

Back in the cellar Cathy stared in horror as the flames around the axe began to splutter and fade. It could only mean Charlie was in trouble, hurt, or even worse. 'Somebody please help us,' she screamed with all her heart.

Her cries echoed unanswered from the dark corners of the cellar.

Chapter 29

Charlie thought he must be dying.

It was a curiously detached thought, as if it belonged to someone else but had been dropped into his head, uninvited.

The pain had actually stopped a few moments ago, reaching such a crescendo that he thought he had heard a pop when all his nerves had simply given up and crept away, leaving him to his misery.

The flames around him were making Beleth's task hard, but slowly and surely they were fading, pulsing in time with his wounded heart. His head rolled to one side and he opened his eyes, just a fraction.

Beyond the violent savagery of Beleth he thought he could see a shape forming out of the distant gloom. Despite the pain that enveloped him, he looked closer, straining his eyes; was that a person? Whoever it was looked familiar as a shadowy form bent over and plucked something from the floor. Beleth didn't seem to have noticed, intent as it was on peeling the last of the protective flames from his skin. The figure was moving faster now, running silently towards them, before bursting into blue flame. There was no longer any doubt in his mind. It was his dad.

Beleth was within inches of victory, the child's throat finally free of flame and ready for its claws. Itching to bathe in the child's hot blood, it didn't sense the presence of the ghostly figure that now stood carefully behind it.

Alex Picker, or at least the essence of him that had endured in this strange wilderness, prepared himself. The amulet and its chain was wrapped around his wrist, its energy reigniting fires around him, fuelling the fragments of him that had been lost in the inter worlds for all these years.

The flames roared from his hands, enveloping Beleth, who had a second to turn and see its attacker, its eyes widening in shock and recognition. It flailed wildly back at Alex, releasing Charlie from its grip and swiping its claws behind it. How could this be? it thought. It had destroyed this Watcher all those years ago in this very place. No human had ever survived in the inter world. The ones that had been brought here had been allowed to wander, lost and weeping with fear, before being hunted, toyed with and eaten. And he had destroyed this one itself, tearing its heart out, killing it. It had been dead, its flames extinguished. Only Beleth was infinite. Humans died, even the Watchers. So how was he here, and how could it stop it? Beleth felt an uncharacteristic twitch of fear. Snarling at the thought, it launched itself at Alex.

Charlie saw Beleth turn to face his dad. He rolled over onto his side, the sudden pressure on his ribs and chest causing exquisite pain. He grimaced, revealing his bloodstained teeth. To his eyes his dad was a strangely ghostly figure. The light he conjured was more vibrant, more present than he was himself, like the fuel was so much weaker than the flame it produced. But he fought so well. He was amazing, moving so quickly, a blur of flame, spearing Beleth this way and that, but he could see increasingly his dad was taking damage of his own.

After a savage period of fighting they circled each other, old boxers buying time, trying to land the knockout blow. Charlie's heart thundered in his chest, each beat hurting him physically, but more so igniting the pain he had been ignoring since his dad had disappeared from his life. He wanted to show his dad that he could help, that he had read his letter and learned his lessons.

Charlie pulled himself to his feet. His head spun at the effort, his heart beating metallic in his throat. His dad was being pushed back, his feet scrambling for purchase. Beleth snarled triumphantly and surged towards him. Charlie drew in a ragged breath. One last push, he thought.

The flames grew from his fingers, powered by the love in his heart for his dad and his mum. For all of his friends. Within seconds Beleth found itself trapped between them. Together they lifted it up into the air within a whirlwind of flame that slowly but surely began to peel away its skin, destroying its flesh, returning it to a formless shape that twisted and writhed in agony. If it wasn't possible to kill it completely then they could at least send it away for a long, long time. One day he would work out how to kill it for good, he thought, even as its screams of rage and pain repeated over and over in his head, the volume diminishing until it was no more than an echo in his mind.

Charlie slumped to the floor. The wounds he had sustained in his shoulder and chest were bad, blood was pouring down his back, soaking his shirt. The final battle had drained the last of his remaining energy. The Beleth had gone and now he wanted to sleep.

'Charlie, wake up,' a voice said. He felt the suggestion of a cool hand on his face. 'Wake up,' the voice insisted. He opened his eyes, but just a crack. A face, so familiar, wavered before him. 'Dad—is that you?' he whispered.

'It's me, Charlie, you've got to get up. You can't stay here. We need to get you home.' He looked up into his dad's blue eyes. Tears doubled his vision. 'Dad, where have you been, why didn't you come back to us? We needed you.'

He felt his dad pick him up, 'Time is short, Charlie, and this is no place for you.' Then softly, a voice drenched in pain and guilt. 'God, you're badly hurt, we need to find a way out.'

Charlie felt as if he was floating, a soft breeze playing over his face. 'Here, this is the spot,' he heard his dad say. He opened his eyes again and saw they had reached one of the thin places. Through the walls he could see a hazy image of the cellar and his mum, and behind her stood Mathilda.

'Dad, what are you doing?' The shadowy figure was unwrapping the chain from his wrist. 'This belongs to you, Charlie. You need to put it back on, without it your wounds...' His dad's voice wavered. 'Your wounds are very bad, you need its protection, its power.'

'But what about you, Dad, what will happen to you?' With his remaining strength Charlie tried to pull away as his dad put the chain and amulet over his head.

'I'll be fine, Charlie. I don't know how but the power of the amulet has let me hold myself here with you. But this is just a moment, an echo. It can't last.' Charlie felt a hand stroke the side of his face, so gently, like a memory from his childhood.

'I did my best. You might not believe it, but I tried. I thought I could match the Nasties, find a way to travel the way they do, through the inter world, to use the amulet and our powers in ways we haven't imagined, so I could finish them for good. I, I failed but, but seeing you again, being me again, even for this few minutes has been so good.'

A single tear shimmered as it slid down his dad's fading face. It was so bright it dazzled Charlie's strained eyes.

'I can't come back with you. I died in here and it's where I have to stay. And that's probably right. I wasn't a good dad, I tried but...but I failed. You and your mum. And that is unforgivable. I'll keep watching out for you, Charlie, but it's time for you to go.'

With the last of his strength Alex lit a flame on his finger, and using it like a knife cut a line through the thin wall that separated the inter world from reality. Charlie could smell the damp earthiness of the cellar and hear the cries of his mum and Mathilda.

'No, please don't go, please, Dad...' he cried.

The faintest of touches guided him through and back to the cold floor. As the walls knitted together Charlie had one last glimpse of his dad. A silhouette outlined in the faintest of blue, and then he was gone.

Chapter 30

The heart monitor beeped out its monotonous rhythm in the darkened room. A nurse bustled past the frosted glass window, soft shoes squeaking her progress down the hallway. Detective Paul Williams slumped further down in his chair. It was impossible to get comfortable, he thought, the cushions were flattened from years of use and the material covering them had worn back to the bare threads. He had been sitting here for days waiting for the man to wake up. He silently prayed for the end of his shift, when he could be released from the cloying stench of disinfectant that sat like a heavy fog over the secure wing of the hospital. Then he would get the hell out of this godforsaken little town. He had grown up somewhere similar and couldn't wait to leave.

The man had been brought into the hospital over two weeks ago. One of the local no-hopers, Duckworth, he thought he was called, had brought the man in suffering from massive trauma wounds. He had been found in Therwick woods not that far from the massacre at the scout camp. Duckworth had not offered up much in the way of a convincing explanation as to how and why he had found him. A hunch, he had said, following a tip-off from an anonymous caller. Those types of coincidences didn't sit well with the senior officers in charge of the Therwick murder investigation. Duckworth, with his white hair and shaking hands, was still being questioned by CID. Whatever had happened out in Therwick woods would reveal itself in time, but for now the sorry looking piece of crap propped up in bed, tubes passing in and out of his heavily bandaged body, was the number one suspect for the murder of at least ten people.

It might be a hospital bed, but the lock on the door and the secure ties at his wrist ensured the man wasn't going very far if he suddenly showed any signs of improvement. As far as Detective Williams was concerned, it was a done deal. His superiors agreed, despite the assertions from Duckworth that the man was the victim not the perpetrator.

The only fly in the ointment, so far at least, was there was no physical evidence connecting Bashir to the crime scenes. Not that this would stop them. In the absence of anything else they had decided that Bashir was their best shot at wrapping up the investigation and going home. When he woke up they were going to nail Pete Bashir. But for now he slept, and Paul Williams's purgatory continued.

Charlie was picking at the plate of food in front of him. He wasn't hungry, but his mum insisted he needed to eat. The wounds on his face and arms had started to heal, rather more quickly than the family doctor had expected judging by his look of surprise when he had changed the bandages that wrapped his upper body. Instead of raw flesh, he had encountered thin pink scars, a puckered rail track that had already spat out the stitches that should have been holding him in one piece. Dr Owen had laughed it off, putting it down to good genetics, but his face wore a troubled look as Charlie pulled his T-shirt back over his head in his consulting room.

The original explanation for the trauma had not sat comfortably with him. Quite how the boy had received such lacerations from a bike accident he didn't know. The explanation Cathy had given was, on face value, plausible but she had studiously avoided his gaze as she told the story. He had been looking after Charlie since he was a chubby baby, and Cathy for many years before that. He thought he had a measure of them both. They were good people. He knew Cathy wouldn't do anything to hurt her son, so he had swallowed the tale with good grace, holding back any searching questions. The wounds though, they haunted him. They had looked like claw marks.

Charlie had been off school for a two weeks now. The 'accident' had brought a few of his friends round, eager for the gory details. They had approved of the heavy bandages and the faint blood stains that seeped out to the edges of the gauze underneath. Mathilda had been round a few times, especially in the first week, when he had been feeling pretty bad. It had been a real challenge to convince her aunt to keep quiet about their little expedition to the woods. Carl had been the key to convincing her. His uniform and the authority that went with it had supplemented his calm assurance that Mathilda was better off being left out of any difficult explanations of what had taken place. Aunt Val had read the papers, they all had, and she knew that Peter Bashir was prime suspect, but she had seen enough damage done to Mathilda in the last few years. Being dragged into the horror of Therwick woods was not going to do her any good. So she kept her silence, although it troubled her mightily to do so.

The flame was still there. The amulet rested under Charlie's skin. He could feel it. There was little doubt the power it generated had assisted his remarkable recovery from the terrible wounds inflicted by the Beleth. When he had slid out of the inter world into the arms of his mum, they had been sure he would die there and then. He had looked like a corpse, but the amulet had started its work, forcing the blood around his body, sealing the lacerations that crisscrossed his skin. By the time they had got him to the doctors, the story they had concocted about a bike accident was at least vaguely plausible.

Seeing Bash was proving very difficult. Carl had forbid Charlie and his mum any contact with him or the hospital. They could not afford anyone making a connection, he had explained. Carl looked strained as he listened patiently to Charlie's furious protests, but in end he had accepted it. He had little choice. The initial cries of outrage in the press had died down a bit, but the embers were still glowing and it would take little to reignite things. Carl provided them with updates on Bash's condition, which were depressing in their brevity. There was no change. He slept on. Charlie thought his amulet might be able to help, it had revived him and he guessed that it might have similar effects if he could get it around Bash's neck. But there was no chance of that. At least not yet. Mathilda had agreed, they would have to wait until an opportunity presented itself. She was confident it would, they just needed to be patient.

His mum had gone back to work this week so the house was quiet. She didn't have a choice. The amount of time she was allowed off to look after him had run out. After that she would not get paid the full amount. The same old problems, bills had to be paid. Charlie thought he could understand a bit better the frustrations his dad must have felt. All the responsibility, all the fear and suffering of being a Watcher and you still had to take your place on the production line. It was little wonder the others had given up. He sometimes felt like giving up too. But two thoughts nagged at him.

The first was a hope. His dad had been alive in there, against all the odds he had survived in the inter world. The amulet had brought him back. Beleth had revealed it had the other amulets, the ones it had taken from the rest of the Watchers. If he could find them, if he could return to the inter world somehow, perhaps he had a chance of saving his dad, of bringing him back to them, so they could be a family again. His dad had hinted as much, suggesting a range of power beyond the basic skills he had mastered. If the Nasties could break through in and out of the inter world, why couldn't he? Maybe there was a way back for his dad.

The second was a fear. That the Beleth would return, or even worse one of the other things he had seen in the shadows of the inter world. The buzzing madness of the things that haunted the darkness still plagued his sleep. He knew he needed to seek out whatever remained of the families, wherever they were. The Beleth had suggested at least one was still alive. If Bash woke up (not if, when, he corrected himself) they would go and find this person. There was still a lot to learn about the power he possessed. Maybe they could add substance to the hopes that his dad had ignited during that achingly short moment they had shared.

But this was all for another time. His normal life called for him. Secondary school, his friends, all the things that had pinned him to the day-to-day he had experienced before the Nasties. Until something changed, or he found a way to force that change, he was stuck. All he could do was wait, and Watch.

Epilogue:

The house was huge and impossibly luxurious. It sat on the cliffs looking out over the vast expanse of blue sea. It had been owned by the head of a local mining corporation, custom built on supposedly protected land, although such restrictions were just a minor inconvenience to the rich and powerful men who exploited the lands of the Northern Territories. That man was gone now. He had left this world begging for mercy, a once proud and ruthless man reduced to a dribbling wreck, ribbons of snot pouring from his nose as he begged for his life.

Warragul, last of the eastern Watchers, sat in a leather chair that undoubtedly cost ten times more than he used to earn in a month working in the mines. He stared blankly out of the huge picture window that framed a swimming pool that looked as if it stretched into the sea itself. An infinity pool, he thought it was called, the height of luxury, although the water was now a dull green instead of its prescribed dazzling blue. He couldn't be bothered to get it cleaned. He never went in it. It was just another empty trophy that did nothing to fill the void in his soul.

Cully had been his only son, his whole life, until they had taken him from him. The official report had said it was an accident, but Warragul knew the truth. It was a truth hard learned by him and all his people. Whatever they said and whatever promises they made, it was always second- or even third-rate justice for his kind. His son had deserved better than being run down in the road like a dog, the drunk driver weaving off from the scene of the accident in broad daylight. Rich and powerful men always found a way around the rules, especially when it was just another Aboriginal kid. He had lost his beloved wife years before and though he couldn't believe it now, he had forgiven that, even when the doctors had looked at him with a barely concealed contempt when he had pushed to find out what exactly went wrong with such a supposedly simple procedure. He had turned the other cheek and forgiven them. But he hadn't been able to do that with his son—not again. He decided he would get the justice his family deserved. He was a man of power, he had watched over them all, protecting them as he was born to do. He and his family had deserved better. And so when the demon had promised him what he wanted, justice for his son and more, so much more, he had embraced the darkness. After generations of service, protecting those that would spit on his family in the street, he had relented and fallen for the promises that rasped into his ear from the broken and bleeding face of the demon, from the broken mouth of the one they called Beleth, the Infinite One. Justice for your son, it promised, riches and power. All you deserved but have never had. Warragul had wept as he made his choice, first embracing the darkness, and then submerging in it for the last four years.

In the darkened cellar of the house something stirred. Warragul heard the noise again, his impassive face twitching slightly at the sound of claws scratching faintly on a tiled floor.

It had returned, broken as once before, flickering in and out of existence as it held grimly to whatever life-force that sustained it. He had thought the nightmare was over, that he had done all that was required of him. He had wanted nothing more than to be left in peace, to mourn his lost life. To disappear. But it had returned. The guttural croak of its voice echoed inside his head, calling him, demanding the food it needed to recover. It was time for him to deliver again—food for the beast.

Printed in Great Britain
by Amazon

10998128R00092